Choice, Set Free
Book 2

The Tae'anaryn
&
the Wizard's Apprentice.

By Dr Joseph Ireland, PhD.

"Dr Joe"

Originally Published by Wombat Books in 2015
Copyright © Dr Joe Ireland, 2014 www.drjoe.id.au
1st edition printed 2014 ISBN: 9781921632914
2nd edition 2015 ISBN: 9781518864780
3rd edition 2018 ISBN: 9781728707891 © 2018
4th edition 2020. ISBN: 9780992329440
5th edition 2024. 9780645899917 in colour
National Library of Australia Cataloguing-in-Publication entry

Author:	Dr Joe Ireland "Dr Joe"
Title:	The tae'anaryn and the wizard's apprentice
Series:	Choice, set free. Book 2.
Imprint:	Dr Joe
ISBN:	9780645899917
Date:	28 December 2020 (current ed 9th July 2024)
Pages:	252
Size:	140mm x 216 mm (5.5 x 8.5 in)
Spine Width:	14.402 mm
Weight:	322gm
Target Audience:	Primary school age. "Middle fiction".
Subjects:	Individuality--Juvenile fiction.
BISAC:	YAF000000 Young adult fiction
Dewey Number:	A823.4 F IRE
Lexile Number:	750

Cover design by Nathan Clark, illustrations by Dr Joseph Ireland

          By Dr Joseph Ireland "Dr Joe"

About the author

I am Dr Joe – Scientist, Author, Edutainer. This means I go around schools and the community helping people to appreciate their world from the perspective of science – and it is a beautiful world, full of wonder, imagination and important questions. But some of the best questions cannot, and maybe never be, answered by science. This is a book that encourages you to ask those kinds of questions.

The Tae'anaryn and the Wizard's Apprentice is a thinking book. It is a book designed to get you thinking, imagining, questioning and exploring your real world from the safety of an imaginary one.

Make the most of every moment, because your life is a precious one, and you have so much to give!

Sincerely,

Dr Joe.

More wonderful titles by Creating Science & Dr Joe:

Choice, set free.

Delightful high fantasy for the thoughtful young reader

1: The Quest of the Tae'anaryn

2: The Tae'anaryn and the Wizard's Apprentice

3: The Tae'anaryn and the Paladin's Squire

4: The Tae'anaryn and the Enchantress's Chrysalis

5: The Tae'anaryn and the Spear of the Troll Prince

6: The Tae'anaryn and the Khozmoh Djinn

7: The Tae'anaryn and the Voyage of Imagination's Dawn

8: The Tae'anaryn and the Crown of the High King

Engaging science fiction adventure with real science!

Space Chase 1: Arrendrallendriania

Space Chase 2: Elizabeth

Space Chase 3: Daniel

Space Chase 4: The Mechanizer

Space Chase 5: Moiya

Space Chase 6: Pancake

Dragon Riders of Pearl

Because Dragons…

Dragon Riders of Pearl 2: Seven Worlds

Dragon Riders of Pearl 3: Return of the Plague

Dragon Riders of Pearl 4: Rage of the Dragonmen

Dragon Riders of Pearl 5: Twilight of the Giants

Trilling young adult science fantasy adventure.

The world's best D&D campaigns – The Wolf in the Sky, Balor's Blade, Quill Versus the Lost Academy of Angelfall, and Hidden city of the Exiles

And don't forget – Creating Science, hands on science experiments and activities for everyone! And Dangerous Science, science to blow your minds.

        By Dr Joseph Ireland "Dr Joe"

Choice, set free 2: The Tae'anaryn and the Wizard's Apprentice

by Dr Joseph Ireland
"Dr Joe"

Dedicated to:

For Rochelle, Andrew, and the entire Manner's clan.
Sweet, wonderful, true believers.

And for Emily Rodda,
Who showed us we could write fun, epic fantasy…
…riddled with riddles.

20-91-5-9   1-8   6-40-1-26

          By Dr Joseph Ireland "Dr Joe"

Contents

Table of Images

         By Dr Joseph Ireland "Dr Joe"

The Riddle

Under the tower, silver and black,
A prisoner waits, her freedoms lack.
A prisoner bold and kind and true,
Protect her heart from darkness new.
The other chained in towers tall,
Bitter, vengeful, darkness fall.
Two prisoners, but one key,
Both are trapped, both to free.
Answers simple; for you see,
The one's chain, the other's key.
When once you know, as so one should,
Knowing evil, yet choosing good.

By Dr Joseph Ireland "Dr Joe"

Glossary

Amicable – friendly.

Crenulations – wiggly bits on the top of a castle wall.

Drudgery – boring, like writing glossaries.

Extinguish – to put out a fire.

Glib – superficial, or with little importance or meaning.

Lenience – to go easy on someone.

immemorial – so long ago no one knows when.

Manifested – to appear. The term is often used to describe what ghosts do when they choose to become visible.

Motif – a repeating design or pattern.

Paralysation – unable to move.

Precipice – a steep and tall cliff face or wall, especially a tall one.

Prudent – a wise and necessary course of action.

Sarcophagus – a kind of coffin where dead bodies are kept.

Serendipitous – fortunate, good. Piex loves using this word.

Scoria – a kind of dark coloured volcanic rock.

Stanza – verses in a poem.

Tantamount – virtually the same as something else, an unnecessarily long word meaning 'the same'.

    By Dr Joseph Ireland "Dr Joe"

The question

What is evil?
– Piex, the Wizard's apprentice.

Kialessa narrowly ducked the rusty scimitars, the goblins shrieking their blood-lusting battle cry as they leapt at her. She tried to trip one with her whip, but it was too quick. She felt the air tingle as Allastassia began to use her sleep enchantment, but one of the little green monsters charged her, breaking her concentration, and was only just kept back by Posk's wild thrusts with his gauntlets. Kialessa cracked her whip to keep the crafty and nimble foe at bay, while Darrix traded blows with the second monster. They were moving in quickly, separating her from her companions with impressive tactical skill. It looked like they might get her this time.

Suddenly the air filled with vivid starlight as Piex unleased his favourite spell all over the goblins. They swayed and fell over.

Kialessa's heart was pounding in her chest at the unwelcomed fright. She *knew* they were only illusions, and that they couldn't do any *real* harm. She knew that she and her four best friends were really in the training ground here at the college. But the goblins still seemed so *real*.

'Great work, Piex,' she breathed, resting a grateful hand on his arm.

'Elementary,' Piex explained, smiling at her with his dragon shaped eyes. He was small for his age, but more than made up for it with his genius at wizardry. 'Goblins might be known for their cunning, but they are still just as susceptible as any knowing creature to *Nethrid's vivid starclash* spell –'

Suddenly Piex stopped short. He was looking down, brow furrowed, as though something bothered him. His clawed hands fiddled with the little tassels at the end of his wizard hat, the way they always did when he was thinking deeply.

'What is it?' she asked.

He paused, tilting his head like he was listening. 'Did you … never mind,' came his cryptic reply.

'Whatever,' Allastassia muttered, probably a little flustered at losing her cool. She was all about being 'cool'; always looking fabulous with her luscious auburn locks and always dressed in the latest fashions. But Allastassia liked to win, and that meant working with only the "best", at least as she saw it. That was why she always worked with Kialessa and Piex when it came to training at the college. 'Let's move on.'

Kialessa smiled, all the usual arguing. King Dunnkan's college, the largest in all the Great Kingdom, held the best training ground for young heroes. Every week brought new challenges, and Kialessa loved these "real life" experiences of plundering far off dungeons or defending themselves from pretended assassins. Having magic about made it all appear so real. It was like living in a fantasy world where you never actually died and got to keep trying until you got it right. Much more fun than real life … at least sometimes.

Next they came to a door and Posk patted it, clenching his gauntlets.

'No, Posk,' she said. 'I'm sure they'd like to keep as many of their doors intact as possible.'

He slunk away from the door with a discontented grumble. Posk was both the youngest, and arguably the strongest student at the college. He was a half troll; green, with a tusk, and insanely strong. Yet he was also seriously mentally handicapped. He had been given the magical door-busting gauntlets by the king after he had helped Kialessa save his life last season.

'Besides,' Allastassia reminded him, 'we're claiming this dungeon in the name of the king. No point damaging his property unless we need to.'

Posk probably didn't know what she was saying, but he always knew when she disapproved. And Posk always seemed willing to do whatever she asked, like most people.

After a careful check, Kialessa opened the door. The next area was set out like a goblin storage room, deep in mountain caves.

'So what do we have here?' Darrix asked. He was, in some ways, the unofficial leader of the group. He was the most popular boy in their year; tall, handsome, the son of a rich merchant. He seemed to know everyone in the castle, and everyone seemed to know him too. But what most people didn't know was that he was one of the most devout and religious people Kialessa knew. He always spent the first and last hour of the day praying, and the high priestess trusted him like no other.

'Look at this,' Piex said, ignoring the crates and piles of rubbish. He went to the far end of the room where there were two bowls set on stands against a blank stone wall. One was filled with water, the other, an olive liquid that burnt constantly, lighting the room.

'What is it?' Kialessa asked.

'Looks like a test,' Allastassia said.

'I bet it's a test,' Piex agreed.

'Do you suppose that there is a door within the wall?' Darrix said.

'Probably,' Piex said. 'I wonder what will happen if we

          By Dr Joseph Ireland "Dr Joe"

put the fire out?'

'I'll do it,' Kialessa said. She scooped up the large water bowl in two hands and flung its contents at the other bowl.

'No, don't!' Piex tried to warn her, but it was too late. The water splashed onto the oil and burst into steam. A column of fire roared up and scorched the ceiling, and large globs of flaming oil leaping out of the bowl, covering her. The four others screamed in surprise and leapt back.

'Ooh, pretty,' Kialessa muttered from among the flames.

'Not like that, Kia!' Piex said. 'The fuel floats on the water. You cannot extinguish an oil fire with water.'

'Oh,' she said, unimpressed, though having grown up in a kitchen she kind of already knew. She watched as the little tufts of flame burnt themselves out on her magical armour, without leaving a mark. She, on the other hand, was fireproof anyway. With red skin, horns, and a tail she was never entirely human, but a Tae'anaryn. Being immune to fire was one of the very few benefits to being one of the most feared and hated races in the world.

'Totally worth it.' She grinned. She placed the oil bowl back down, and it was already full again with burning oil.

'Then how do we put out this fire, Piex? I don't have much mastery of fire, and I suspect that's how we pass the test,' Allastassia said.

'I agree, but Allastassia, enchantments aren't needed here. Fires need live air; stale air extinguishes them. We just need to block off the normal air.'

Allastassia looked around to see what might do that.

Kialessa tried her hands, but the fire kept sneaking out of the edges and spaces between her fingers. 'Nope,' she declared.

Darrix spoke up, 'How about we empty out the water bowl and put it on top of the fire bowl; let it smother the flames.'

'Oh, good idea, Darrix,' Piex said.

'All right then,' Kialessa said, and put the dripping water bowl over the fire bowl. 'Goodbye, little fire.'

As the two bowls pressed together they clicked in place, setting off the opening mechanism on the secret door that was, indeed, hidden in the wall.

'Impressive; I highly doubt goblins could have developed such wizardry. These caves must have once held other occupants. May I suggest –' Piex began to explain to no one in particular.

'Oh, look at that!' Kialessa cut him off. A section of the wall had slid across to reveal a small cavern, and inside, an open chest. It was ornate and well made, and contained a shining sword on top of a small pile of treasure.

'Wait!' Piex called.

They waited in silence.

'What is it, Piex?' Allastassia said in an impatient voice.

'Did you … I'm sorry, did you hear someone?'

'I heard you tell us to wait,' Allastassia complained.

'What is it, Piex?' Kialessa asked, resting her hand on his arm in an attempt to encourage him to speak.

'I heard someone say something. Like "impressive".'

'Oh please, that's probably just the sagemaster checking on our progress. You must just be picking up on his scrying sensor.' Allastassia huffed, and went with the others to examine the cavern carefully before touching any treasure.

Piex laughed a false and hollow laugh. 'Yeah, probably.'

Then he turned to Kialessa and whispered so that only she would hear, 'But my wizarding master doesn't *have* a scrying sensor, not to my knowledge.' He looked at her, concern written all over his face.

'Don't worry about it,' she said, since there didn't seem to be anything they could do about it anyway. 'The tutors are always checking up on us. If your master created this dungeon, he'll be able to see into it, right?'

'Hmm, you're probably right.'

They went into the little room, Piex standing by the door so that he could leap in or out in an emergency.

'I cannot sense any danger,' Darrix said, 'Kialessa?'

'Looks clean to me –' she began.

Suddenly another illusionary creature leapt at them, not from the chest, but from the shadows at the edge of the room. It was bloated and muscular, a toad the size of a large dog. It sprang towards them. Darrix dodged it at the last instant.

'Gross!' Allastassia screamed.

Darrix struck at the toad, but his sword had barely pierced the creature's thick skin before it jumped up into a corner of the room near the roof where it clung to a small ledge. An instant later, its tongue shot out and lifted him up off the floor by his throat – it was surprisingly strong for its size. Posk leapt up at the toad, but he could not jump high enough, and sparks flew as his gauntlets scraped along the wall.

'Help me!' Darrix choked. His sword and shield clattered to the floor and he grabbed the toad's powerful jaws and rammed them shut, battling to keep them closed while it struggled to swallow him.

Kialessa shot an arrow at the toad but it dodged, still clinging to the roof. It dragged the struggling young warrior to the corner where it could better avoid their attacks.

Allastassia spoke some kind of magic, but it did not seem to affect the toad. 'This creature does not hear me!' she wailed.

Posk grabbed Darrix's sword but could not get a clear attack as the toad swung the young man around. The toad was using Darrix like a shield while trying to position him just right for swallowing him whole.

Kialessa squealed in frustration, not sure what to do, when suddenly a magical ray of freezing ice raced past her and shot the toad right on its head.

It let out a croak of surprise and fright, but didn't drop

the warrior. Instead, it hid further in the corner. Piex shot it again, and it finally dropped Darrix to the ground. He landed in a crooked sprawl on top of Posk.

The bloated toad took one leap over their heads and began to retreat rapidly from the room, down the way they'd come.

'Quick, Kia, shoot it!' Piex said, working on another spell.

But she did not. Instead, she helped Darrix to his feet and let the toad flee.

'Leave it be,' Darrix said as he stood, breathing in new air from being almost crushed by toad jaws. The illusions didn't really hurt, but they could still be uncomfortably realistic.

'What?' Piex said. 'No, it's getting away!'

'Leave it,' Darrix repeated.

'What? Why?' Piex demanded.

'Because it's defeated, why destroy it? Further violence has no use,' Darrix said.

Piex was not satisfied. 'But what if it returns with friends? Or what if it breeds? All giant toads are evil.'

'Evil?' Kialessa said in disbelief. 'Just because they're giant toads doesn't automatically make them *evil*, does it?'

'Maybe not for you, you're a tae'anaryn,' Piex protested, 'but toads can't think. They just consume. If not Darrix today, it'd be some other wretched soul. Don't you think it would be better to destroy them all when we have the chance?'

'Actually, I think *that* would be evil,' the enchantress disagreed with him as well. 'Just hunting it down because of what it is? That sounds evil to me.'

Piex was alone in his opinion.

'But … what about using its body for spell components?' He argued forlornly.

'Oh! Now that *is* evil.' Kia laughed with a kind smile.

The others weren't interested in the argument anymore. They were already gathering up the treasure, Posk running it through his fingers while Allastassia tried to stop him so she could organise it better.

'But then what *is* evil?' Piex pondered out loud.

No one seemed to pay him any attention, until suddenly he gasped out loud, and clutching his temples fell to one knee.

'Piex, are you all right?' Kialessa rushed to his side.

'Yeah, yeah. I'm fine,' he lied. Then he whispered again, a genuine tremor in his voice, 'You didn't hear someone?'

Kialessa shrugged.

'Whatever. I just must be imagining things.' He smiled, and looked at her, his face a thin mask that hid an expression of pity and fear.

***

In a tower far away, a powerful archmage was watching.

'Such talent!' The archmage said. 'Far in excess of what that so-called college can ever teach him. Something *must* be done …'

1 You... didn't hear someone?

The day the wizard went away

Be strong in adversity. Sometimes the hardest thing to do, that requires the greatest strength, is not to fight, or even to flee … but to comply.
– Prayoth, High Priest of Serros at Emerel.

Kialessa watched as Piex's eyes filled with tears, and his bottom lip quivered. She had gone with him to the wizard's study and watched while they spoke. There, the old elf had some bad news.

'What do you mean, sagemaster De'Feur?' Piex finally said, voice choking.

The old elven wizard sighed, his purple eyes betraying a touch of sorrow. 'I have to go away for a half season,' the wizarding master repeated in a kind tone,

     By Dr Joseph Ireland "Dr Joe"

looking out the window while he spoke in Emerellian so that Kialessa could understand. 'There is an important elven ceremony that I must attend. But you will be well tutored while I am gone, and if it interests you, I have arranged for you to have access to my personal section in the library.'

He waved his hand, and in a moment, his purple pocket dragon uncurled from around his hat, leaping from chair to bookshelf, where it held out a little gold key to Piex. Any other day, the apprentice wizard might have lost his breath with excitement at receiving it. As it was, it appeared he valued the wizard's company more than the wizard's books. But he took the key with politeness.

He brushed away his little silver tears. 'You will return soon then?' He asked.

The old elf sighed once more. 'Most likely. Mother has many ambitions at this time of year, and it is an important time for we elves to meet. It might take some time.'

Piex said no more, and ran from the study.

The wizard shook his head. 'A young wizard …' he began, but left his lecture unfinished. Wizards rarely showed emotion, at least the ones Kialessa had met. While he clearly expected Piex to show the same composure, Piex was still very young.

The sagemaster sighed again, packing books into his magical satchel. 'Watch over him, Kialessa. This is an important time for him. He will try to lose himself in the books, to forget his sorrow, but I fear he may also forget his friends. Leave him there for a time and watch for when he longs to emerge, then help him find his way outside the library once more.' He turned around to place a gentle hand on her shoulder. 'He will need a good friend like you at this time.'

Kialessa nodded. She watched as the little pocket dragon curled up on the wizard's hat, chittering in anticipation.

The sagemaster cleared his throat authoritatively. 'Well, that was the last goodbye. Till next season,' he said, and sweeping up his glowing amethyst staff, he teleported away with a soft *whoosh.*

It's amazing how he makes it look so easy, Kialessa thought.

***

Piex didn't turn up that afternoon for studies of athletics and physical prowess. He didn't turn up that afternoon for archery. Kialessa knew he'd be in big trouble for that. He'd probably get detention. But being in detention meant he could still read college books, and she knew there was nothing he'd like more.

Sure enough, he got detention. Still, another two weeks went by while Kialessa waited. She barely saw him, and when she did he was reading. When he spoke it was only to say "yes" or "no". He even took to reading his books during other classes, but since he'd memorised almost everything they tried to teach at the college, few tutors were upset by this. Soon they stopped giving him detention and let him sit in the library every day. People started to forget he was even there.

But Kialessa didn't; it was like losing a friend.

Over the days she grew more and more worried for him. By the third week her heart was particularly heavy with concern for him. Her head was down as she clutched her books to her chest, walking along with all the others to their next class.

'He's grieving,' Darrix said, seeming to know what she was thinking. 'He feels he's lost something.'

'How long can a person grieve?' Kialessa asked.

'A very long time, it seems. I think you'd better go talk to him.'

'I've tried. All he ever does is say yes, or no, or nothing at all.'

'Well you've got to speak to him,' Allastassia said. 'We've not gotten into the finals against the senior students for three weeks. I don't know what he does, but we need him.'

'I … I'll try again,' Kialessa agreed with reluctance, not only because she didn't like losing to the bossy senior students, but because she cared about Piex. So she skipped lunch and went to find him.

She found him quite easily, deep in the castle library, hidden within the locked section and studying intensely. He looked at each page for only a few instants before turning it, as was his way.

'Just getting the feel for the book before reading?' She asked, hoping he'd talk to her.

'No,' he said. 'I'm reading every word, very quickly, and I remember them all. I can do that. But this little wizard's band that the master loaned me helps,' he said, pointing at the rune encrusted band of pure silver on his head that had replaced the apprentice wizard's hat that he'd made himself long ago. The headband was a rare prize, designed to improve focus and intellect. But still, he'd sounded so sorry that his mouth didn't even bother trying to smile.

'Planning to read them all before he gets back?' she asked. There were at least two hundred books there.

He looked up at her without smiling. 'I'm almost done.'

*That's a **lot** of books*, she thought.

She could tell he didn't want to talk, but at the same time, he really needed to. She thought about asking him to help in the next challenge against the senior students, but then realised he probably didn't want to be needed, at least not while his feelings were hurt.

But he couldn't stay in the library alone. He needed to conquer his fears so that when the castle wizard returned he would see a healthy and eager young student, not a frightened boy who'd hid in a library until he returned.

Why is he hiding? Kialessa wondered. 'You miss the wizard?'

    By Dr Joseph Ireland "Dr Joe"

He thrust the book shut and glared up at her. 'It's not fair! I'm the best student he's ever had – he said so. I only *just* got to work with him and he takes off.'

'He'll be back,' she said, but Piex went quiet again. She wondered if she had upset him. Perhaps some feelings weren't for solving, they were just for hearing.

'I know you're the best student he's ever had,' she said, changing the subject back to what he seemed to want to talk about. 'You're the smartest person I've ever met.'

It worked.

'He's got six other students, the most he'll ever take, but all they do are boring sigils and low-level prestidigitations. None of them have any *real* talent. Even Marchan, who's been practicing for *seven years*, can barely conjure mage's momentum dampening body armour. Master De'Feur says Marchan will be in his old age before he can cast the fiery conflagration. He's only good for wizard chores. The only reason he's a wizard at all is because his parents are rich and want a wizard in the family to help run their noble estate.' Piex kicked the air in his bitterness.

'Who, the sagemaster?' Kialessa asked.

'No, Marchan!' he said, hitting a book. But he was smiling. Piex seemed to enjoy being angry for a change instead of being sullen and silent. Perhaps this was progress? Kialessa didn't know what to say, so she stayed quiet until he felt the need to fill the silence.

'Master tells me I've talent to exceed him. He expects

me to be able to teach him magic one day.' Piex's voice was sad.

So how could that be bad news? 'That's good,' Kialessa said.

Piex looked up, sorrow in his eyes. 'Then why did he go away? If I'm so talented, wouldn't he want to spend as much time as possible helping me practice, instead of reading books? I love books, but I can read books in my own time. I was reading books long before I finally got to work with a real wizard. It's not fair.'

At last Kialessa felt like she was beginning to understand. Piex didn't feel challenged by books. What he wanted was a chance to test and improve his skill with a greater wizard who could guide him and tutor him personally, to give him the special attention that he craved. But was he being just a little … spoilt. Even travelling wizards had little time to instruct apprentices. His master would return. Surely a half season to study would be a chance to prove himself, not punish himself and disappoint his master?

'How can I help you make the most of this opportunity?' She said after a while.

'Hrumph,' he said, lip pouting. 'What I really need is a powerful wizard who'll take me under his wing and show me deeper magic. That's what I need.'

Kialessa knew history talked about many powerful wizards, but not all were good. 'Be careful what you wish for,' she quoted the athletics teacher.

It made Piex smile.

'Your master will return,' she said, 'and when he does, you can show him what you've learnt. Impress him. See it as a test of your ability to learn things he hasn't taught you, things he cannot teach you!'

Piex sat up, grabbing a book as his face lit up with his growing enthusiasm. 'I have learnt several things,' he said. 'There's this one point about ice magic in *Glacius Maul's third treatise on low temperature magic* that I think he missed out on from his comments made during his appraisal of my casting *Kreegon's inimitable temperature declivity*, my ice ray, the other day during training. I want to know if he's heard about it.'

She joined his smile. 'C'mon, Piex, let's get you into the sun. We've lost the last two challenges with the senior students. They're starting to say they should have caught those thieves themselves.'

Piex looked ashamed. 'I've been hiding.'

'You'll never change the world unless you live a little.'

'Actually,' he disagreed in a good-natured tone while packing up his books, 'it's quite possible. Disintegrees managed to discover a whole class of levitation spells without casting a single enchantment, he just pieced together the research of several other sages!'

'Well, you'll never change the world unless you leave the library.'

'Once again,' he said, smiling, 'Elf-sage Fuoco DiFiume was able to fight an entire army of trolls, using nightmare magics conjured entirely –'

'Oh stop that,' she said with a smile. Kialessa had realised long ago that there were two kinds of people you couldn't win an argument with: those who knew too much, and those whose arguments were based entirely on personal belief. Piex, it seemed, was the former.

He picked up an extra-large book and finally looked ready to leave. It was his first spell book, the one that was a special gift from King Dunnkan for helping Kialessa to save his life a few weeks ago. It was coloured a deep mahogany, bound in leather with a proud display of Piex's family crest in gold on the cover.

'How's your research going?' she asked.

'I've finished transferring all my spells now. But there are a few spells he had scribed for me that that I can't decipher yet. So I'm hoping to work out what they are before –'

In the next moment they both flinched involuntary as there was a huge explosion from outside. Kialessa heard people screaming and saw guards began running down the hall. Piex and Kialessa ran to the window.

'It's an attack!' Piex cried in alarm and disbelief. Two enormous black griffons with massive troll spearmen mounted on them tore down from the sky and pinned the guards at the entrance of the large courtyard just outside the window. The guard's arrows bounced ineffectively against the griffon's thick armour, and the beasts tore the weapons from the soldier's hands. The castle guards were clearly outmatched.

Suddenly there was a terrifying screech from the sky. Piex covered his ears and everyone ducked. A moment later, an even larger creature descended from the clouds. It had deep green and black scales, and a mass of what appeared to be rotting vegetation for a mane. It had bat like wings and an enormous snake like tail that trailed behind it. From its emaciated torso four hideously clawed limbs set down on the grass, turning it black as the soil clogged up with brackish swamp water, and dank moss sprang up on the nearby walls.

A rot dragon.

It roared again, and in its presence the guards fled shrieking, as did everyone in the library. Everyone except a little dragon boy who was too terrified to move, and his tae'anaryn friend that would not leave his side.

'Impressive,' Kialessa muttered.

The rot dragon was as tall as the library roof, but moved as swiftly as a snake under the midday sun. A rider leapt down from the black leather saddle on its back. He too, had wings, and was looking around at the courtyard as if trying to find something.

'Kialessa, run.' Piex trembled.

'I'm not leaving you.'

'That dragon. Its screech … it was calling out my name in Dragonspeech,' he said, trembling with terror.

It seemed impossible to believe.

'*Operari*,' she said. Immediately, her college clothes

folded up, and in their place, soft fireproof leather armour adorned her. She unfolded the whip from its hook on her belt.

'If he comes for you, he comes for me,' she promised, unafraid of what the dragon could do to her in the king's college.

The winged stranger looked up at the window from some distance away. He was wearing a dark mask and a black robe that flowed around him with sharp marks of glistening silver down the front. His hands gently glowed with black and silver arcane fire.

Then, with a gesture so sudden it was difficult to perceive, he made all the stones in the wall crumble and rot away in an instant. A gust of wind struck her, bringing the rich, deep smell of fetid vegetation: the scent of the dragon, no doubt. Without waiting another moment, the black and silver wizard cast another spell and began gliding effortlessly towards the window.

'Piex, come with me,' he said in a coarse and gravel voice, like a dragon's. 'I have come to teach you the true way to magical power.'

Oh look, Piex, you got your wish! Kialessa thought to herself.

'Who … who are you gentle?' Piex pled, hiding behind her. The Piex she'd known at the start of the year would have fled crying already. But the dragon boy crouched behind her, his first spellbook clutched protectively to his chest, and was talking to this powerful wizard who somehow knew his name.

Anyway, thought Kialessa, *from wizards as powerful as this, where is there for apprentice wizards to run?*

Slowly the wizard removed his mask. His skin was covered in dark blue and silver scales, and one eye was bleeding black tears. His tongue was cloven and his face stretched out like a crocodile's. He was a half dragon.

'I am your Uncle Tobiuus, the archmage.'

'Great Uncle Tobiuus!' Piex muttered in fear. 'Father told me you were imprisoned for using necromantic magic.'

'Your Father is a fool who knows **nothing** of power! He has squandered your talent in some college when you should be mastering the arcane truths of the universe! Come with me, Piex. Only *I* can teach you your true destiny and power.'

Piex trembled as he clutched Kialessa's armour.

'Never,' he whispered, so quietly only Kialessa could hear it.

'What?' his uncle roared.

'Never,' Piex shouted in a faltering voice. 'You killed innocent –'

Tobiuus smiled. 'It doesn't matter. You are coming anyway. Once you taste the true strength of the power you possess you will soon be convinced. Things are changing in the Great Kingdom. You must come with me.'

Kialessa cracked her whip, dimly wondering why she wasn't afraid of this half dragon wizard. 'If you want Piex, you'll have to take me first,' she said.

He looked at her in surprise, then his mouth contorted into an evil smile.

'Very well then.' He made a simple gesture, like he was pulling a little splinter from her eye.

She heard his voice inside her mind, as if it was as if it was part of her. It told her to climb out the window and get onto the back of Txlax, the rot dragon. She watched, far away as if it was a dream, and her body obeyed that voice and began taking her over the grass towards the rot dragon. She heard Tobiuus mocking as she went.

'I have taken command of the simple young mind of that friend of yours, Piex, and she will be a servant at *my* college of magic.' He laughed. 'So unless you want to see her turned into another one of my experiments, I suggest you follow her example.'

She could hear Piex calling after her, screaming her name, but her body and mind were no longer her own. She hardly even felt a twinge of fear as she walked up to the massive creature, didn't notice as it bent down to help her climb up, didn't smile as she took the saddle and held on with unnatural calmness.

Some part inside was screaming to be free, but it didn't know how.

Crying great tears of sorrow and clutching his only spell book, Piex took his uncle's arm and allowed himself to be lifted over to where the dragon was waiting.

'It's not your fault,' he sobbed in Kialessa's ear. 'I

forgive you. It's not your fault.'

She said nothing. She couldn't. She did not even look at him as the impressive black creature took to the air. An instant later the king's honour guard, who did not fear dragons, burst into the courtyard just in time to see the tae'anaryn and wizard's apprentice lifted high into the air on the back of the rot dragon. Uncle Tobiuus threw a bolt of silver lightning, scattering the guard. The courtyard echoed with his cruel laughter as they disappeared into the clouds, away from the safety of the king's college.

Of black and silver

There is no evil; no dark, no light. Only an infinite number of shadows.

– Teaching of Bgrethol, high cleric of Pumos.

Kialessa was silent as they flew west over the western forests and well beyond the troll infested highlands, almost to the Broadwater river that divided the Kingdom of Lenmer'el from the greater troll lands.

After several hours of frigid silence in the clouds they finally began to descend towards a fog laden swamp. There, in towards what must have been the centre, a tall tower waited. Its dark, foreboding crenulations were topped with polished silver, and a strange black and silver symbol in the shape of a lightning bolt adorned every wall. It seemed that in the years since his escape

     By Dr Joseph Ireland "Dr Joe"

from prison Uncle Tobiuus had built a haven of secret wizardry, and it was to this place that they were taken. The tower was surrounded by a deep and rotting swamp where the evil rot dragon no doubt hunted. Fuelled by unparalleled cruelty, he would be the perfect way to keep anyone escaping from the tower.

As soon as they landed Tobiuus dismissed his mental control. 'Now listen closely children. This is your home now. Piex, you are now one of my apprentices and will be trained in all my knowledge. If you listen well, you will prosper. If not, well, I'm sure you are a studious boy and we won't have to worry about that; your father was not *entirely* bereft of talent.'

'What about me!?!' Kialessa asked as she gained control of her mind and body again. She was glad Piex had someone to help him through this, but she couldn't believe they'd just been kidnapped and forced to attend a new college less than two seasons since she'd started attending her first! King Dunnkan would stop at nothing to find them. She couldn't wait to see the look on Tobiuus's face the day that happened.

Uncle Tobiuus glared at her and then answered as if Piex had asked the question. 'Having someone to witness your rise to power will be fitting, and a companion to be awed by your mastery is always … satisfying. If the tae'anaryn is your choice of companion, then so be it. However, she is to remain silent at all times when in my presence, on pain of being turned into a toad and used for *soup*. She is at no time to address me directly. Is that clear, Piex?'

'Yes, honoured,' Piex agreed in his most polite voice and without hesitation, begging her with a quick glance to be silent.

Kialessa simmered in anger, but knew better than to challenge the wizard today. One would have to be a complete fool to not see that Tobiuus was a very powerful archmage.

The next moment goblins hobbled up the stairs. They were even more repulsive and frightening in real life, their sly eyes glinting with hidden mischief. Never more was she aware of their reputation for filth and cruel humour. They joined them on the roof, standing tall and quiet. They were just a little shorter than Kialessa, and Piex moved to stand behind her.

'You'll find goblins quite obedient, when it suits them,' Tobiuus said to him. 'A while ago I saved their king from a great misfortune, and they came to serve me out of gratitude. Be sure to listen to them, as they know the routine. And make sure your tae'anaryn follows their example.'

The goblins looked at them and seemed unimpressed. They held their heads high with the professional bearing of well-trained servants.

A moment later Tobiuus mounted his dragon. 'Be ready to begin your studies in the morning, nephew. Further instructions are on your desk.'

As soon as he was out of sight, the professional bearing of the goblins melted, and they leered at them with greedy hunger in their eyes.

'This would make a nice breakfast,' one of them said, saliva dripping from his chin.

'I like tail,' another agreed, reaching out a grubby hand at Kialessa.

'Stop that!' She shouted and spun around so fast that it didn't have time to move before she'd slapped its hand away. The other cowardly goblins took a quick step back.

Another laughed. 'Mmm, feisty.'

Piex clung to her tightly.

2 Atop the tower

'Stop that, or my wizard will turn you into stone!' she threatened them, knowing only a fool would believe that such wizardry was within Piex's level of skill at this young age.

Thankfully, it seemed the goblins were fools. They shut up completely. With a begrudging, yet silent wave of its hand, one of the goblins led them down towards a dark, polished doorway. He held a magically burning torch to light the way. They moved along several flights of expertly cut stairs towards a series of doors where, presumably, the apprentices studied. The whole tower was dark, but neat and well organised. It was highlighted inside with silver doorhandles and frames, and some of the works of art were very beautiful.

But it was still a prison.

'What do you think he's going to do with you?' Kialessa asked Piex as they followed the goblin. No doubt the apprentice wizards became fit walking up and down these stairs several times a day.

'He wants to teach me his evil magic,' Piex said with a tremor. 'Oh, Kialessa, we have to find a way to escape!'

'Yes, but not now,' she whispered, not knowing how good goblin hearing was.

'When?' he whispered in desperation.

'Soon,' she said, but she didn't know when. Somehow, they would find the right time to escape.

The goblin, who had said nothing as he led them down the stairwell, gestured with his magically burning torch at a wooden door with a symbol that Kialessa didn't recognise on it.

'Twelve,' Piex interpreted. Kialessa went to open the

door, but hesitated as she felt a sizzling crackle of static electricity as she approached.

The goblin laughed. 'Yes, Master is wise. Only the apprentices may open their doors, see? We servants are not permitted –'

'Servant?' Kialessa interrupted.

'Yes.' The goblin laughed, happy to see her discomfort at that suggestion. 'That is why the master brought you, yes? You are his apprentice's servant? No others are allowed.' He sounded apologetic, but was clearly enjoying making them uncomfortable. 'I hope I have said nothing out of place?' He crooned and smiled wickedly, displaying his grimy, pointy teeth in the dim light.

Piex looked disgusted, and went to shove the door. It swung open before he'd touched it.

'Watch your tongue goblin, or I'll freeze it off,' he said in an angry voice.

'Ahh, so much like the master, you sound,' the goblin mewed, being very sarcastic, 'it marinates my heart to hear you so take after him!'

'Get out,' Kialessa said. The goblin pretended to show respect by bowing, then walked away, smug goblin laughter echoing through the halls.

The room beyond was excessively neat. It had a soft feather mattress bed, a sturdy oak desk, and wardrobe so large it could not have fit through the doors. There was also a pile of straw covered by a thin blanket, resting by a warm fireplace. The whole room was decorated in Uncle

Tobiuus favourite colours: black and silver.

'Oh, they wouldn't!' Piex said in disbelief.

'What?' Kialessa asked, looking around.

'Here,' he offered, 'you sleep on the bed; I'll sleep on the straw.'

Then she saw it; there was only enough bedding for one. Servants had no place to sleep other than on a thin pile of straw.

But Kialessa had grown up on straw by a fireplace, and the king's mattress had not softened her that much.

'Really Piex, do you think your uncle would allow it? Wizards need their sleep. Besides, I don't mind. I've slept on straw for most of my life and it's nicer than a mattress in many ways.'

He still looked terribly guilty. 'I … I cannot believe I dragged you into this.'

'You didn't. Tobiuus enspelled me, remember?'

'Yes, yes he did.' Piex reminded himself.

'It seems he likes an audience and wants his apprentice to have one as well.'

'Apprentices. That sigil on the door indicated that I'm one of twelve.'

Kialessa hadn't thought of that. 'That's a lot of apprentices. Why would he want that many?'

'It could be a casting circle, but I won't know until we figure out what he is planning. I don't know. Maybe he just likes apprentices?' he said, a touch of hope in his voice, but then he cried, 'Oh, how do we escape?'

     By Dr Joseph Ireland "Dr Joe"

'We don't. At least, not yet. Calm down, Piex. The time will come. For now, let's make the most of it!' She walked over to the straw and wondered how she might arrange it for bedding. It wasn't much; it was probably only used to start the fires.

He did not look convinced or happy.

Then he burst into tears.

'I want to go home,' he wailed. He sat on the bed and cried for a good ten moments, while Kialessa patted him on the back and at first tried to cheer him up, but it seemed better to let him cry.

Now they really were prisoners, but at least the jailor wasn't going to hurt them. At least, she didn't *think* Uncle Tobiuus was going to hurt them …

Somehow they would be rescued, or find a way to escape.

***

The next morning the goblin came to their room to fetch them. Kialessa had managed to get Piex to read out loud the entire list of castle rules his uncle had left on the desk, which were many. They prepared her hair the way he'd been instructed, but she kept her leather armour on for safety.

Kialessa convinced Piex that, for now, they needed to play along. They had to learn all they could about everything and wait for their chance to escape. They decided not to talk too much, since there were probably spies hidden in the room, ready to tell on them. It might have been a ghost, a goblin turned into a desk, or any number of things. And the less Uncle Tobiuus knew about them the safer they felt.

They followed the goblin up to the breakfast room where the other eleven apprentices were eating their food. All of them had a servant to assist them. Kialessa saw a lot of goblins, but there was also a strange creature made of wood and stone, a small troll, and two grubby and nasty looking human slaves.

Of course, Kialessa was not to speak to the wizards under any circumstance. All their servants were as rude and bossy as the wizards, even the humans, and they did not like to share resources with the other servants. She almost had to fight one to get a plate for Piex. None of the servants looked happy, even the strange wood and stone creature. It was an automaton that stood silently by the dark robed boy who sat at the head of the table, a silver circlet on his brow. All the other wizards deferred to him. They called him Dusk.

As soon as Piex walked in, Dusk eyed him with dark and threatening suspicion. He spent most of his meal levitating food into his mouth, leaving his knife and fork clean beside his plate. The other wizards jumped at his command, giving him everything he demanded.

'Steer clear of that one,' Kialessa mumbled to Piex.

He heartily agreed.

Breakfast was noisy and disorganised, but brief. As soon as the bell rang, breakfast was over, and the wizards all hastened out with their servants.

They rushed up a flight of stairs and around a corner into a great chamber. Piex and Kialessa followed behind, hoping they were going in the right direction.

Uncle Tobiuus stood in the centre of the room.

Morning studies had begun.

The apprentice wizards formed a semi-circle in front of him, their servants stood at the wall behind their masters. Uncle Tobiuus began by citing an oath in a language Kialessa didn't recognise. Then he asked some of the apprentice's questions, and if they did not answer well he glowered in disapproval.

Then he spoke in Emerellian so that everyone would understand. 'I expect you to welcome our new student, Piex. Although he is my nephew, my brother's grandson, he can expect no preferential treatment from me, and I expect no preferential attention from any of you,' he warned. 'He has some talent and will no doubt supplant several of you within the first few weeks, so be sure you study hard. Piex, welcome. Oh, and he has a tae'anaryn servant.' Tobiuus added as an afterthought.

'Welcome,' the students muttered.

Piex nodded. She could tell he didn't feel welcome.

'I trust,' his uncle threatened him, 'that we can expect your best while you are studying here? Any breaches in protocol, or lapses in excellence, will be dealt with *most strictly.'*

'I understand,' Piex said, his voice cold and obedient.

The other students looked surprised. Dusk raised an eyebrow. They could tell Piex didn't want to be here. Perhaps he had given away too much already?

'All students will continue their studies with the first apprentice immediately. I have important research to attend to myself. I will see you all for the evening report.' He nodded, and the students left.

'So he's not even going to teach me himself,' Piex murmured. 'Just use another apprentice, typical. I can guess how this will end.'

Not very well, Kialessa thought to herself, and the guess seemed spot on. Dusk was a spiteful and impatient teacher, who used a stick to hit every student who failed his tests. Piex, under that motivation, learnt quickly, and was clearly the envy of all other students who did not pick up the learning so well. She knew enough about wizardry from the college to tell it was a lesson on Undanium spells, yet it was all held in Dragonspeech so that Kialessa and the other servants could understand virtually nothing.

But Kialessa found it informative to watch the other servants. She could tell the wizards took no notice of their servants, but the servants took keen notice of their masters. Indeed, she quickly perceived that some wizards were so dependent on their servants they would soon forget how to look after themselves entirely.

Kialessa was interrupted in the middle of those

thoughts as Dusk hit Piex with the rod. She tried not to jump into his defence.

'W ... with all respect, first apprentice,' Piex stammered in Emerellian, holding his swelling hand, 'but the correct order of incantation for the spell you speak really is *eye, doh, ney.*'

'That is not correct.' Dusk insisted, his voice calm, but his eyes flashing with anger. He raised the rod again. 'Now, if you do not get the order of incantations for the spell I will be forced to strike you again.'

'Perhaps if you would peruse a casting scroll with me?' Piex said, temerity in his voice.

'I have no need to.'

Piex sighed, and restated the spell the way Dusk preferred it, but rebellion was written all over his face.

*****

Later, at the evening meal, Piex was angry.

'Dusk is a fool! He has **half** the wizardry I have.'

The wound on his hand was light, but it would still make casting painful. And they'd put salt on it too, to ward off infections. It had hurt.

'Why's he the first apprentice then?' Kialessa asked.

Piex grumbled. 'He's actually quite accomplished. I wouldn't want to meet him in combat, but his wizardry is lacking.'

So Piex was again being taught by inferior students of

magic. Only this time they insisted by the end of a rod that he learn their incorrect ways. She watched as Piex simmered, mumbling his discontent until the evening report.

Kialessa hoped he'd gotten over his anger, but she was wrong.

It happened some time towards the end, as students gave their report and demonstrated their skill with the day's training. It sounded like Piex had asked a question. It was a simple question, but Tobiuus grew angry. He shot several quick comments at Dusk, who answered unsatisfactorily.

Without moving his hands, a twisting, deep green bolt of lightning shot out from the air in front of Tobiuus and struck Dusk in the chest. He fell over, wheezing.

'A simple reminder that failure is not tolerated at this college,' Tobiuus said. The other apprentices looked at Dusk in fear and alarm, but did not move. The wounded apprentice stumbled to his feet and tried his best to stand up.

'What was that?' Kialessa whispered to Piex.

'Necromantics. The spell drains strength, but should wear off in a few hours.' Piex whispered back.

'There is no shortcut to **excellence**!' Tobiuus shouted. 'Only hard, dedicated work. There can be no mistakes, as a single miscast spell can mean your *life*. There can be no compensation for such failure, for we are toying with the primal forces of the universe! I want only to bring out your best, and those who will not abide by my standards will falter and *fail*.'

The students were silent.

With a grunt, he dismissed them all.

Kialessa turned to Piex, waiting for their chance to leave. He was smiling to himself, but holding his wounded hand close. Kialessa began to fear this magic college might bring out his worst.

'What's Necromantics again?' she asked as they waited their turn to leave.

'It's one of the eight halls of magic.'

'I know, but which one is it? I mean, what were they?'

'Well, all of knowledge is like a huge mansion with eight great halls, or maybe like spokes on a wheel. There's Praesidium, the hall of protection; mage's momentum dampening body armour is based on the physics of Praesidium magic. Inflornium, for finding things out; very useful. Then there's Necromantics –'

'Not you, Piex, come with me.' Tobiuus's voice suddenly called out.

Piex looked up alarm.

Kialessa held his uninjured hand and encouraged him. This was not the time to disagree with his uncle.

Tobiuus turned and walked up another two flights of steps, where they followed him into his personal study. The walls were hard stone, encrusted with sigils of power and covered with the scorch marks of past battles or experiments that had ended in near catastrophes. Half the room was covered in rigidly catalogued bookshelves. There was a long bench along one wall, and several cupboards full of various potions and oozes. At the far end, under stained glass windows, sat a large stone desk. On it was a strange bird, like a crow, only with bright iridescent feathers. It sat tethered by a delicate silver chain to the desk under the bright colours of the window.

'This is a great privilege. Usually only the first three apprentices see my work in this study.' Tobiuus muttered, seeming to speak only to himself.

Piex grimaced.

Kialessa could tell that he did not want to see his uncle's work in this study.

'There is something I want you to learn,' Tobiuus said in a stern voice. 'Something your father never taught you. For example, you see this creature?' He gestured at the strange bird and stroked it kindly.

It did not return that kindness and may have even trembled under his touch.

'Would you like to see what it can do?' he asked.

Tobiuus nodded at the bird, and with seeming reluctance, but very quickly, it changed its shape into a small cat.

They were amazed.

'This is no ordinary bird, methinks,' Piex said.

'Can you guess its origins?' his uncle asked.

'Have you enspelled your familiar to be able to shape shift? I sensed no illusions.'

          By Dr Joseph Ireland "Dr Joe"

'Very good, youngling.' Yet from his lips the term 'youngling' sounded more like an insult than a term he would use in kindness. 'No, this is no familiar spirit, for I take none. This is an imp from the lower realms.'

Piex leapt back, but Kialessa didn't know enough to be afraid.

Tobiuus laughed.

'You do well to fear them, youngling. A creature of this kind, unshackled, could best both of you in battle, no doubt. Their poison is fast enough.'

'Why do you keep an imp?' Piex said, his voice trembling.

The little cat hissed at him.

'Why not?' His uncle laughed. 'Because from it I can gain great knowledge, and knowledge is power, and power is why we became wizards, is it not? Besides, this creature amuses me. It often tries to escape.'

'But it is evil,' Piex protested.

'That it is. Wholly and completely; but we have no need to fear it. Can you tell me why?'

Piex studied the creature with care. 'All I see is a silver chain holding it to the desk. Is it strengthened with Praesidium magic?'

'Well done again. See, the chain is held on by the slightest knot, but it is more than enough to hold this creature to my will. You see, it has been blessed by the most holy of priests, and filled with goodness till the creature cannot break it. A creature which, mind you, would cause no end of ill in the world if it were to be released.' Tobiuus laughed.

The cat looked up at Kialessa, who had drawn closer, with sorrow and pity in its eyes. Then it shifted to form a perfect miniature image of her, and poked out its tongue at her. Kialessa stuck her tongue back, and the imp looked surprised. Then it shifted into a pitiful miniature goblin, and held out its hands towards her, tugging the little silver chain at its feet.

'Be warned, Piex,' Tobiuus said. 'Should your witless servant release this imp, the first thing it will do is destroy her.'

'Oh, it wouldn't,' Kialessa began, but the imp turned into a cat again, and tried to scratch her. Its paw landed on her outstretched hand, but the marks were light. Either its real claws were too small or it didn't *really* want to scratch her.

'Witless servant,' Tobiuus muttered, and stared hard at the imp until it shrank back again into the corner. 'Show us your true form,' he whispered.

The imp muttered something in a strange, vulgar sounding language but Tobiuus scowled. Whimpering, it changed.

It had a body similar to a human's, but it was a deep red, with bat like wings and a forked tail. On its head, a pair of tiny horns about the same size and shape as Kialessa's resided. And on its face there was a wicked smile. Kialessa could feel the unshackled mischief

        By Dr Joseph Ireland "Dr Joe"

emanating from it.

Kialessa's first thought was, *Well, it may look a little like me, but it is nothing like me on the inside.*

'Why do you keep such a thing?' Piex said, stepping further back.

'Piex, you must not fear evil,' Tobiuus instructed, reaching out and grabbing him by the arm, forcing him closer to the imp, 'for this is why I have brought you here. In evil, as in goodness, there is *power.*'

'That I do not doubt,' Piex said, trembling. 'But not the kind of power I would embrace.'

'Then you are a fool, and the son of a fool. Your father had this weakness also. He could not see that there was power in sin, just as there is power in righteousness. Real power: true power, lies in maintaining that balance. The exact balance between good and evil, between creation and destruction, pleasure and suffering. I am one of the few mages who truly embrace this truth, living on the fulcrum of eternity. **Behold**!'

A great flame of terrible, flickering colours leapt up from his left hand. It radiated darkness and fear, and screams of suffering seemed to be echoing in its wicked light. The air went cold, and dimmed the light of hope in Kialessa's heart.

Tobiuus laughed, but was concentrating deeply on his craft. The colours swirled and merged, becoming a pure darkness akin to the blackest night.

'What is it?' She dared to whisper to Piex.

'Evil energy,' Piex said fearfully. 'Manifested wickedness. With it, he can bring disease, wound his enemies, drain their life force, he can even … create undead.'

'As he has done before,' Kialessa whispered, 'and was that why he was sent to prison?'

'He took the bodies of those he killed and brought them back to life as undead zombies in his service.'

'*Behold*,' Tobiuus roared again. 'The fulcrum of eternity!'

From his right hand a great silver flame sprung up, a blazing array of power and hope. It seemed to be composed of health and courage itself.

'Good energy?' Kialessa asked.

'Or something like it, I thought it was white,' Piex muttered.

Uncle Tobiuus struggled as he brought the two flames close. They roared and fought against each other, threatening to break out and consume the archmage in their conflict. The imp watched with interest. By supreme effort of mental power, the archmage harnessed the energies and forged them into a solid shape: the lightning bolt symbol that was strewn all over his tower.

He breathed deeply, seeming pleased with himself. 'It is done, once more. The balance of good and evil in the world is maintained. You too, must master this balance.'

Piex was visibly awed by his uncle's mastery. 'But evil energy only causes suffering.'

'That may be so, but so do swords and bows, and no soldier is hauled off to prison just for wielding them. You must embrace sin so as to comprehend goodness.'

Piex was silent.

'Hmmm,' said Kialessa, talking as though to Piex, though knowing that Tobiuus would hear. 'I don't believe that power is found through balancing good with evil. Goodness respects the balance in nature, evil strives to upset that balance.' It was the kind of thing Kialessa and Darrix used to debate at the shine of the Eternal on Serrosday.

'Do you not see?' Tobiuus said, driven to distraction by his utter conviction in his own logic. 'Without death there can be no life. Without sound there can be no silence. Without destruction, there would be nowhere to build … there *must* be good and evil, and when you harness them both –'

'He is being deceived,' Kialessa said to Piex, not sure why Tobiuus seemed more interested in debates than being obeyed at the moment. 'One cannot turn to evil to learn the truth about goodness, because evil always lies. Only goodness will tell the truth about evil or goodness.'

'But what is evil then?' Tobiuus said, a crafty smile on his eager lips.

Kialessa would have spoken, but found she had nothing to say. "Doing bad things" didn't sound right.

'Then this is your first riddle, Piex. Tell me, for I know you have been asking: what is evil? Tell me this, and I'll let you study however you choose. Tell me, and I might even let you go.'

Piex said nothing.

Kialessa was silent.

'Go,' Tobiuus ordered. 'I will teach you nothing more today.'

Figure 3 Archmage Tobiuus, Piex' grand uncle

        By Dr Joseph Ireland "Dr Joe"

Wizardry

My only regret is not trying something new, every day.
– Anon. cited in 'Recollections of the tae'anaryl.'

'Magic isn't easy,' Piex suddenly blurted out.

One week had passed and they were mopping the kitchen floor again. The goblins were all too lazy and

Dusk had just decided it was Piex's turn. Perhaps it was punishment for a mispronounced sigil? Perhaps Piex had challenged his authority again? Perhaps Dusk was just a tyrant.

Kialessa wondered what was wrong. 'I know magic is diff –' she began.

'You have to learn a lot of words, and what they mean,' he interrupted. 'Trouble is, most wizards don't *actually* know what they mean,' he complained.

'What do *you* mean?' she said, resting on her mop.

'Even the greatest sages are often just guessing. A total of four hundred- and sixty-words sigils have been officially uncovered, and everything else has been created or guessed. It's not easy to do magic, you know.'

She just listened.

'Every now and then some scholar hits on a new word or phrase left over by the Ancients. It turns out a thousand words can be summed up in a single phrase! Then, here's the sore part, *they don't tell anyone*! All these secrets; no one talking. Who knows what forgotten secrets Tobiuus has uncovered, but he's not going to share them.'

He paused, then continued softly. 'I mean, the right word would just clean up this whole mess, but we don't know what it is.'

Oh, she realised, *he's complaining about cleaning up. Another job beneath the dignity of your average wizard's apprentice.*

'You're more like your uncle than you realise.'

He looked at her as if he didn't understand what she meant.

'Teach me magic,' she said.

'You? I ...'

'Please?'

'I'm only just teaching you how to read, and you want to learn Dragonspeech?' He sighed.

'Please?' she begged, not only because she wanted to stop having to listen to him complain, but because she really wanted to learn. She thought it was amazing watching the wizard's practice. She had only just begun to realise wizardry was something she wished she understood as well.

He kept on working. 'We'll, it's not like witchcraft, I can tell you *that*!' he mumbled something unintelligible about his uncle's teaching. 'All prayers and wishes to demons or any god who might hear... No! Wizardry is a *science*, with strict laws governed by mathematical logic. It draws on natural law of the physical universe, once understood properly. It takes years to master, years!'

'We'll we'd better start soon then,' she teased him.

He looked at her sideways, as if trying to decide if she was really being sincere. Then he shrugged. 'Magic isn't easy. Look, the first thing you have to do is promise me you'll never tell anyone what you learn. These secrets are for wizards only. I don't know why they make us promise that, but every wizard swears an oath to keep the secrets, so you have to promise. I think it has something to do with the power of our words.'

'I'll keep your secrets, but I'm not going to make an oath.'

'Meh, good enough for me,' he said. 'Now, everyone has magic, and wizardry helps us to harness those powers. I know I complain about the words, but they still work. At least we wizards have some explanations for what we do, even if it's explanations we've created for ourselves. You see, Academiclees taught that everything has a pure, divine essence; a perfect form that exists in Creation. And each essence has a corresponding symbol and a sound, a word, which can be used to access the pure essence by wizards here. Got that? Now, the first magic word of power …' he paused, getting closer to her, 'is *Ecce*.'

'*Ecce*?' she said, then gasped. Suddenly the air twingled around her as it filled with magical energy. She'd felt that before, but never coming from within her, from her own words. She ran a curious hand through the magic around her in quiet wonder.

'It means, well, we think it means "the power is here". Or "put the power here", or "see the power here". Something, because all the magic flows … hey, are you alright?'

Kialessa could feel the magic in the air around her. It seemed so familiar, as if it had been there her whole life but she'd never paid enough attention to notice. She wanted to shape it, give it life. Yet at the same time, as it responded to her thoughts, it guided her actions, and she knew that there were possibilities inside it that she had never imagined. It was like a fire inside, threatening to burst out of control.

'Just relax Kialessa. Not a very common reaction, but you are a tae'anaryn. They often have sorcerer powers, you know. Actually, I am surprised you haven't manifested any sorcerer powers yet.'

'What's a sorcerer?' she demanded to know, the forcefulness of her own voice startling her.

'They are a little like enchanters in some ways, except they draw on evil sources to fuel their magic,' he said, brow furrowed.

'Evil?' Kialessa's voice surprised even her with its demanding tone. 'What is it with you people and tae'anaryl? Just because of the colour of my skin you think I've some kind of natural inclination to evil!'

'No, no, I don't think that.'

Her magical aura reached out to envelope him, and she felt the magic around him. It was as if he was covered with tiny little motes of light, especially in his hands and around his head, all invisible to the eye. The light seemed to be symbols or words, each holding great power and great potential. Perhaps he had placed them there during his many years of wizard training. Although she could see nothing, it was as if his mind was a blazing furnace of infinite possibilities. It was beautiful.

'*Ponere*,' he said, stroking her arm.

Instantly she calmed down, her energy obeying his authoritative command. But the energy was still around her.

'Take a couple of deep breaths. You alright?'

'Yes,' she said, not sure if she was. She was trying to be calm, but deep inside she felt a terrible desire for more power.

'You went kind of weird for a moment there. Maybe you've a talent for wizardry. Well, I suppose we can find out. Now you know the first word of magic, and most wizards make their apprentices wait four years before teaching them that! I'll show you how to write it later. Here's an easy one, say *Ignis*.'

'*Ignis*,' she repeated, but felt nothing.

'We think that means fire. Now when you join the first word with the word for fire you create 'great fire'. But even that's not noticeable. What you need to do is double the fire. *Ignis geminis*. Then repeat it ten times and you have a great fire over a thousand times what you originally began with. Let's see if you can create the fire finger.'

'All right.' She smiled. '*Ecce, ignis geniminis, ignis geniminis, ignis geniminis, ignis geniminis, ignis geniminis, ignis geniminis, ignis geniminis,* no wonder spells take so long to cast. *Ignis geniminis, ignis geniminis, ignis geniminis, ignis geniminis.*'

She felt magical energy condensing around her, gathering and gathering. Nothing happened, though Piex seemed pleased.

'Now, to unleash the gathered energy you need one more phrase, a key phrase that unlocks the gathering powers and tells them what to do and when. In the case of finger fire you simply need to tell the fire where to go, and that phrase is "fire finger", or *"ignis digitus"*.'

'*Ignis didgitis,*' she cried, and the outstretched finger burst into flames.

Kialessa was just beginning to celebrate when she noticed all her other fingers were on fire as well. 'Hey, look at this.'

'Oh, that's unusual. Maybe your race has a particular aptitude for fire? You'll need to be more specific about which finger to gather the energy on. That doesn't happen to half dragons and humans.'

'Cool!' she said, but then noticed the fire was going out.

'Fire finger will probably last longer once you're not diluting its power over all five fingers. I'm glad you didn't overdo it. A few more doublings and your whole body might have burst into flame!'

He smiled like it was a joke, but Kialessa wanted to try it.

'You've performed a spell that usually takes weeks in under five moments,' he muttered. 'Your ability to draw on the magic around and within you grows with experience, but you seem particularly adept. Now, once you summon the spell's energy your body will hold on to it almost indefinitely until you use the command word, such as *ignis digitus*.'

'So if I prepare a fire finger, I can cast it any time?'

'Yes! Well, no. Well, I shouldn't be teaching you magic. We'd better get back to work.'

But Kialessa was just beginning.

'Is there a word for "clean up"?'

'*Purgo*,' he said, mopping. 'Though I think it might also mean "set right". Still, no wizard will give you both meanings though, and it's not going to help much in this situation without a proper algorithm …'

He continued to mutter, but Kialessa wasn't listening. She called the magic to her. She called for cleaning. She doubled it and doubled it. Then she touched the broom.

For a brief moment it twitched sideways, sweeping the floor.

'… always picking on their students,' Piex muttered, 'when they are just as ignorant …'

He didn't notice, but she didn't care. She wanted to see what her magic could do. This time, she didn't need to set up the energy. It was already there. So she doubled it. Again and again and again until the mop leapt up alive and moved on its own.

'Hey, check this out,' Kialessa said.

Piex jumped. 'Did you do that?'

'I think I did.'

'What were the words you used for animation, or balance, or the program to have it rinse itself like that?'

'I have no idea!' She smiled.

'That's … not a good thing,' he said. 'It's like sorcery. You need to stop it. You need to stop it *now*, Kialessa.'

'But I want to get the floor clean,' Kialessa said, even though she knew it wasn't true. She wanted power. She wanted to see what she could do. She wanted magic so she could burst out of this prison. Piex has lots of power. She could have power like his.

'We'll be fine,' she said, and laid a comforting hand on his arm.

Suddenly she felt full of power, the room shining with motes of magic.

Piex yelled out, and thrust her hand away, almost collapsing.

'What are you doing?' he said in alarm.

'I'm cleaning,' she replied, ignoring him. 'Clean, clean, clean.'

He was shouting, or he might not have been. But it didn't matter now. She had all the power she needed. The mops could wash the floor; the towels could wipe the benches. She could just dance around and bring them all to life with magic!

She looked at the sink. So many messy dishes to clean! But what if they could clean themselves? What if they could all be set right? Double clean, double clean, double, double, double again!

It was like music in her head as she danced around, bringing the room to life. The clothes folded and packed themselves, the spices jumped back into their racks. The cutlery walked into the sink, the brushes scrubbed them and then they walked themselves right into the cutlery draw. It was real wizardry!

She looked at Piex, and he stared around in amazement.

He'd be pleased with her now.

Then she saw the door. It was just a little off its hinges. It was messy too.

Well, we can't have mess like that in a wizard's tower, she thought, and a moment later the door tore itself off its hinges and crashed to the floor. A pair of pliers from the bottom drawn walked out and began straightening them. This would be the neatest door in the castle!

She sung among the cacophony of motion as the room set itself right.

Piex ducked and dodged the whirlwind of crockery as it cleaned and organised itself.

Clean and clean and double clean!

A pair of goblins walked by, probably to see what all the noise was, and stared in amazement at the dancing furniture and the little wizard waving his arms around in the midst of it all.

A pair of dirty, stinky goblins.

Well, I can certainly fix that.

The dish clothes whisked across the room and wrapped themselves around the smelly little goblins. They cried out in dismay as they were dumped in the sink, spoons and dishes dodged aside to let them pass. Their terrible screaming, as they were scrubbed and washed by animated sponges, was only barely drowned out by the crashing of mops and dustpans that ran across the room, wall to wall.

Walls.

The walls were filthy too. *How could a wizard work like this? Dirty, dirty wall. We'd better fix them too.*

One by one, the bricks started pulling themselves from the wall. Suddenly she began to feel tired again. A few mops and brooms sagged in their duties. She'd need more magic if she wanted to clean the whole tower.

Bells started to join her chorus. Was it an alarm? An instant later Dusk rushed in and attacked the tools.

How rude!

Then his automaton started hitting bricks. An automaton full of magic. Magic she could use …

Without a sound she walked towards the automaton, walking right past Dusk, who ignored her and shouted something at Piex, something that sounded like, 'Stop that now'.

She touched the automaton. It was *full* of magic! Dusk had done a good job of building it and implanting magic deep into the wood and stone. Its power would last for hours. Its power would be enough to rip every brick from this tower and scrub it till it shined!

Tobiuus might not think I'm good at much, thought Kialessa, *but I do know how to clean!*

'*Placidus*,' she heard a voice mutter in her ear. It was Piex. The magic around her dissipated, but just a little. He'd need a thousand more like that to pierce her magic! And he was starting to look a little dirty too.

But something in his words touched a part of her soul that must have gone to sleep. She looked into the room with new eyes, and saw it for what it was. Brooms and dishes spun out of control, smashing and chipping into each other, water spilled from the sink all over the floor. One by one, bricks fell from the wall, creating a dangerous hole in the side of Tobiuus' tower.

It was a disaster.

'Stop. *Stop*!' she said.

But the magic was out of control now. Stuck to the automaton, her powerful, magnified enchantments kept growing.

'Stop,' she yelled, and wrestled a broom to the floor. But it flung her off and kept mopping. Bowls and brooms wacked against her, ignoring her in their magically compelled flight to clean everything. Every person, every stone.

They wacked into her, striking her face and hands. She stumbled backwards and raised her arms to protect her face, and in the next moment found she had nowhere to go. The bricks had broken away from the wall. She was standing at the edge, looking down the cliff-like precipice of the enormous tower. From across the room she saw an enormous dustbin, overflowing with rubbish and broken bricks. It was rushing towards her.

Suddenly it crashed to the floor, rubbish spilled out over her feet. Every broom and dish cloth slopped to the floor. The goblins in the sink fell silent.

Tobiuus stood at the door. He had uttered a single word that she did not hear. He surveyed the wreckage darkly, his heels cracking against chipped and broken plates as he entered the room.

Dusk was looking at his automaton, shaking its sleepy arm with a confused look on his face.

Piex was sitting in the middle of the room, a mop resting on his head.

Tobiuus glowered down at him.

Piex removed the mop.

And with a wry smile, a smile which seemed to say, *I am proud of you, but you did wrong*, Tobiuus slapped Piex on the back of his head.

Evidently, Tobiuus had decided it was Piex who'd lost control of his magic in an attempt circumvent his chores. Tobiuus walked out, his laughter echoing in the halls.

Nothing more was ever said of the event, and Kialessa and Piex never got dish duty again.

Kialessa didn't practice her wizardry much in the coming weeks, but she paid a lot more attention to what was going on during the classes.

Conspiracy

Sometimes you must wait for change. Other times, it's up to you to make the change you wait to see.
- Plarros, 6th sage of Lumos, keeper of times.

It had been a fascinating four weeks, but Kialessa was getting tired of waiting for their rescue. She was beginning to wonder where King Dunnkan and his honour guard were. Did the sagemaster know they'd been kidnapped? What was being done about saving them?

That night, Kialessa decided they'd waited long enough.

'Piex,' she whispered. 'I think it's time we tried to find our own way out.'

'Are you kidding?' He shook his head. 'The tower is

surrounded by a swamp. We have to find our way through that without the rot dragon noticing, and even if we did, the hills are crawling with troll hunters. How would we ever get past them?'

'Look, I'm sure Tobiuus has some kind of scrying protection on his tower, or someone would have found us by now.'

'That's a good point.'

'So even if we get only a little way out, at least it would give them a chance. Besides, I think I'd rather take my chance with the trolls than another of your uncle's "punishments".'

'He does enjoy it, doesn't he?' Piex said. That morning he'd copped a mind addling spell which had ruined his casting for more than two hours. Piex was still embarrassed. 'But I still don't think you should try. It's hopeless.'

And that was all the convincing she needed.

'All right,' she lied to him. 'You go to sleep while I polish your boots. We'll wait a few more days and see what happens.'

'Thank you.' He flung himself back on his bed, sighing.

He just doesn't know how to take risks, she concluded.

That night it was as dark as scoria outside, thick clouds covering the moon and stars. Kialessa knew the goblins could see perfectly in the darkness, so she had to walk as quietly as the moon, yet without a light. It wasn't too hard,

Tobiuus had many burning torches along the walls of his castle, and their light spread far enough that there wasn't any place where she couldn't see where she was going. She pulled open the study door with a stick and stepped out into the hall, making sure it was open just the tiniest bit so that she could get back in once she'd finished looking around.

The tower was surrounded by a swamp, and to get down to the swamp, she had to find a way out of the tower. She went by the back door to the apprentices' study rooms and down the long flight of inner steps that joined every level of the tower. It took a long time as she slipped past dozens of goblins, all too lazy or busy to notice her. And even if they had, she would have walked right past them like she was supposed to have been there, and they probably wouldn't have known the difference.

She reached the lower levels, where the goblin kitchens were. There were only a few goblins now, throwing out food and doing a poor job of cleaning. They were speaking to each other in their coarse language and Kialessa couldn't understand a word they were saying.

Just then she heard another goblin coming down the stairs. She slipped into the kitchen just as it hobbled past her, carrying a huge load of dishes from dinner. The goblins shouted at each other for a moment, then the unlucky goblin was forced to wash up all the dishes on its own.

And as he did he was scraping the food into a large

rubbish bin.

Where does the rubbish go? Kialessa wondered.

An idea was forming in Kialessa's mind. Ten moments later he tipped the whole lot of rubbish down a chute and it disappeared into the darkness.

A moment later the goblin finally finished and left, grumbling bitterly as it went. She was getting stiff legs, but couldn't risk trying to escape when it might see her. It extinguished the lights and the fire then headed out, scraping and nattering as it went. Kialessa waited until its voice was gone before she crept from her hiding place and went to the shoot. She opened it and the rancid smell of the swamp drifted up.

It was a way out.

Kialessa was about to start heading back up when she heard footsteps descending the stairs. She hid again as quickly as she could.

However, this was not the clatter of goblin boots, but the steady pacing of wizard's shoes. Kialessa hid as best she could as a bobbing globe of floating light made its way down the stairs. It was followed by Dusk, the first apprentice, the little glowing ball of blue to guide his way.

He walked right past the kitchen, much to Kialessa's relief. She was about the go up the stairs again when curiosity began to nag her. *What is he doing down here so late? Is he hiding something? Perhaps it is something useful.*

In spite of her better judgement, she followed him, without making a sound. He walked right around to the other room at the lowest level of the tower. It was filled with crates and shelves.

He reached the far end of the room and looked about him, as though searching for onlookers. Kialessa froze as he looked right in her direction, but he did not appear to see her.

'*Aperire,*' he said in a language that she didn't know, probably Dragonspeech. The stones in the storeroom floor began to fold out and down, making themselves into a crude staircase.

Dusk headed down the staircase and began talking. A goblin replied. She did not know what they were saying, but she had to wait only two moments before he returned. As he left, the staircase reformed into a floor.

Kialessa really wanted to see what was in that room, but was too nervous about the goblin finding out that she was down here. She repeated the strange password a hundred times inside her head to help her remember it for later, just in case. She would still have to think of a way to get past the goblin if she did want to find out.

But even more than that, she wanted to escape. She wanted to tell someone about Tobiuus's terrible tower and where he lived. Then they would take him away and lock him up forever.

***

Kialessa told Piex all about what she had found out

the next day in the most secret place they knew: the crowded and busy breakfast table.

He almost choked with surprise. 'I can't believe –'

She cut him off; she wanted their conversation to appear completely natural. He laughed in a terrible attempt to make everything seem all right.

'I can't believe you snuck out and didn't get caught!' he whispered.

'Nothing to it,' she said, handing him his fork. 'What do you suppose that other room underneath the storage room is?'

'It must be the dungeon where he keeps his experiments, and his most important prisoners. We don't want to know what horrors live down there.'

'Fair enough, but I also have a plan for escape,' she told him like it was old, unimportant news. 'We'll wait till dark and let ourselves down the shoot in the kitchen, then we just have to find our way out across the swamp and we'll be free.'

Piex thought about this, then answered, 'My uncle sends out for supplies about once a week, and a large cart cuts across the swamp. If the dragon is out, maybe we can get past it safely by catching a ride on the cart?'

'It's worth a try. When do you think we'll get our first opportunity?'

'With luck, soon.'

As luck would have it, they got their first opportunity the following night. Dusk informed them all to have their requests for magical research equipment ready by that evening, and Tobiuus had already left with his dragon on a journey. Kialessa and Piex tried not to look too excited.

That night the kitchen was busy for a long time. They hid behind some barrels and made as little noise as possible. Piex almost fell asleep several times while they waited in the darkness for the goblins to stop, but eventually the room fell silent and they left their hiding space.

They'd torn up Piex's bed sheets to form a kind of rope and lowered it down the rubbish shoot. Piex climbed out first, but it wasn't until he was near the bottom that, to her dismay, Kialessa discovered their rope was too short.

'Don't worry, there's a pile of rubbish to soften the landing,' she told him.

'What?' his disbelieving voice whispered. 'I'm not going to jump onto rubbish.'

'Don't worry, it's just below you. Can't you see it?'

'What? No. Just get another blanket!'

'We can't get another blanket,' she said, exasperated. 'Just let go.'

'I'm *not* going to let go.'

But she couldn't pull him back in, he was too heavy. And he couldn't climb back up, he was too weak. So she did the only sensible thing there was to do.

She dropped him.

He squeaked as he fell the remaining few paces onto a pile of rubbish. Swamp lizards went sloshing in all directions to get out of his way.

'Are you all right?' she asked.

'All right? Of course I'm *not* all right,' his angry voice whispered from the garbage.

He was all right.

She was about to climb down the blanket too when she realised a little flaw in their plans. The goblins would see their "rope" and know how they'd escaped. So she untied it and let it fall to the ground.

'What are you doing?' Piex said as the rope fell to the ground, probably afraid he might be left alone.

'Don't worry,' she replied and began climbing down the walls as best she could. There were large stone blocks with wide gaps between them, much easier than athletics class back at the college. She could probably climb all the way to the top if she wanted to. By the time she'd let herself down to the ground Piex had wiped most of the gunk off himself with the sheet rope.

'You look disgusting,' she teased him.

He gave her an angry look. 'C'mon, let's go.'

The carriage was waiting outside the gates. Kialessa led their way across the damp soil and climbed in the back with no trouble at all. She helped Piex hide inside, and together they waited out the half hour before the goblin drivers came back and started the journey out through the swamp.

The path criss-crossed in a haphazard way through the darkness. Slowly Tobiuus's tower grew smaller as it faded into the distance. Too slowly. But as the hours passed, the cries of Txlax's children, the young dragons, grew more and more distant. The goblins were chatting in the front when Piex gasped.

'What is it?' she dared to whisper.

'They're taking us to a troll village! We can't go there.'

'Don't worry, let's get out here.'

She tried to open the carriage doors but they were bolted from the outside. So she tied some thread around a nail and used it to pull the latch outside. With great care, she opened the door and slipped out onto the carriage plank. Piex was next, but gasped when he saw that he'd have to jump. She motioned for him to go first, but he shook his head.

She insisted, but he pleaded with his eyes. She showed him her fist and made her eyes glow.

So he shut his eyes, and jumped.

She hadn't really meant for him to do it that way, but it worked. The loud thump he made as he hit the ground and bounced around fortunately didn't alert the chatty goblins in the front. She relocked the carriage and jumped down to the ground without harm.

'How do you do that?' Piex asked her as he ran to catch up, breathing hard. 'Always land on your feet?'

She smiled. 'How do you master wizardry?'

He smiled. They were both good at different things.

'Now,' she said, 'let's get as much distance between us and that terrible tower as possible.'

They walked for the rest of the night, stopping only for a few hours in the boughs of some long dead swamp tree, cuddling together for warmth. Little insects kept biting them, and Kialessa wasn't sure if they had slept at all. At first light they started out again, but soon lost the road in the dark and confusing swamp. Often they found themselves sloshing through knee deep mud to get to where they wanted to go, their only source of navigation the dim moon in the sky.

The sun was just coming up as they left the swamp and ran for joy in the dark grasses that lined it. The tower had dissolved into the mists of the swamp long ago and Kialessa began to wonder if there was any tower there at all. Perhaps that was how everyone saw the swamp?

Piex sat down.

'I think I need a rest,' he said out loud, admitting his exhaustion for the first time.

She pulled him up. 'Nope. Let's use the daylight to get as much distance between us and that tower as possible.'

Piex complained, but admitted the wisdom in her plan. They did not stop again till lunch, and made their way up a large hill to see where they were.

To their intense disappointment, it was mountains all the way to the horizon and beyond.

'It did not seem that far when we were on the dragon,' Piex moaned.

'It'll take weeks to pass all this,' Kialessa said, 'and we only brought enough food for a day.'

'What do you think we should do?' Piex's voice heavy with regret.

'I think –'

Suddenly they heard a great screech of a dragon from the sky.

'Run,' she screamed, and begun taking flight down the mountain.

'Hide,' Piex called after her.

But she was already caught up in her sprint, running for her life, determined not to be caught by a dragon. But she had barely gone a hundred paces before it landed right in front of her.

It was Txlax, Tobiuus's favourite dragon.

It eyed her with savage hunger. 'You should have hidden when your wizard told you to,' it said, vicious teeth gnashing like they'd rather be gnawing on her bones. 'Then it would have taken me five more instants to catch you. You know, Tobiuus lets me eat them sometimes; the students that fail.'

The dragon laughed.

'Please don't,' she pleaded.

'I should,' it roared, and snatched her up in a single claw. Another three wing beats and it had grabbed Piex too. Kialessa banged against its claws, punching them with her tired, frustrated fists. She looked at Piex, who lay still in the claws, resignation written all over his face.

He sighed. 'At least we might get dinner.'

		By Dr Joseph Ireland "Dr Joe"

***

To their surprise Tobiuus didn't seem angry at all.

'Well done,' he said after they'd been plonked back onto the roof of his tower. 'Your escape from my fortress has highlighted several important lapses in security that I had not noticed. Now, I trust you will resume your studies as planned?'

'Yes, sir,' Piex agreed, picking himself up from the floor.

Tobiuus continued with a stern glare. 'As for you, tae'anaryn. Don't lead my apprentice off on any worthless adventures ever again. What you do with your life is your business, and if you wish to lose it trying to escape, that is your choice. But he has his studies to attend to and you are not to distract him ever again. Understood?'

She said nothing.

'Understood?' He roared.

'I thought I wasn't supposed to talk to you,' she said, knowing that she was being defiant.

Tobiuus looked livid for a moment, then laughed again, 'You've quite the wit, tae'anaryn girl. You will serve my apprentice very well, if you live. But know this, if you continue to lead him astray, or any others, you will suffer a great penalty. I will *not* warn you again.'

His voice was stern and threatening, but Kialessa sensed there was still something he was afraid of, or that he was hiding from them. She began to wonder what it might be and found she only had more questions. Why did he force Piex to be his apprentice? Surely it wasn't just to teach him magic. The college was doing as good a job as any at that.

It must have been to teach him how to be evil. Why? What did he need? If Piex became an evil wizard, did it justify what Tobiuus had done somehow?

'What I want to know is why?' she asked boldly.

Tobiuus glared at her.

'Why do you need Piex?'

'I see no need to answer you, servant, but since it may serve my apprentice very well, there is a good reason. Long ago I tried to teach his father my wisdom, but he rejected my tuition. Now he is a mediocre sage of little importance. Once I saw what great talent Piex held, I knew he needed to be taught by only the best. So I have brought him here to become the best wizard he can be. That is why, to make sure the errors of his father's ways are not repeated.'

'My father is a good man!' Piex said.

'That he is,' Tobiuus agreed. 'But that is *all* he is. He failed to embrace true power of harnessing both good and evil. You *must* embrace evil as well as good, or you will never become the mighty wizard fate has intended you become.'

'I will never make evil my ally,' Piex promised.

Tobiuus laughed as though he didn't believe him. 'Then you will never know power.'

'There is power in goodness too, even more than in evil!' Kialessa said.

Tobiuus stood up, enjoying this debate every bit as much as Piex might if he were not forced to make life altering choices by it. 'It is true,' Tobiuus lectured, 'if all the powers of evil swarmed out into this world they would destroy it. But I assure you that it would be just as much a catastrophe if the powers of goodness took over here too. All that is evil they would burn up, and of those left they would no longer be free to choose, knowing only good, and suppressed into the way of being of the angels.'

'That is foolishness,' Kialessa said, filled with indignation and inspiration, not knowing what to say before she'd said it. 'Good people respect other people's right to choose, unlike evil people. So if the angels did take over, they wouldn't take away our freedom to choose. They haven't yet, and who's to say they do not fight every hour for our right to choose anyway, even if it is to choose evil, like you do!'

'Evil is not the only path of power; you will soon learn. I have done much of what you might consider "good" in my days. I have found the cures to numerous poisons, I have unlocked several enchantments to break mentiantic magics.'

'Looking for redemption?'

His eyes lit up in anger. 'I need no redemption, or forgiveness, for there is none. Only power, and those willing to move on from their mistakes. Now, I make very few mistakes.'

And with that, he turned Kialessa into a toad.

'Contemplate your insolent tongue for the next day, tae'anaryn. And you, Piex, pick up your servant before she becomes the next meal for my goblins.'

Piex did not let her go at all for the next day, hiding her inside his robes until she turned into a tae'anaryn again. She could not be more grateful, because although her mind was still fully hers, her body was entirely toad. It was torturous to be so slow moving and helpless. The only kindness was that toads do not cry, so no one could see her weep over her hopeless imprisonment, and her anger and fear of the powerful archmage that kept them there.

        By Dr Joseph Ireland "Dr Joe"

Dragon training

Enough goodness can counteract any evil in the world, and kindness is a balm to sin.
– Prayoth, High Priest of Serros at Emerel.

The days moved on. Piex rose quickly to become the seventh apprentice, and his new personal study room was much larger, with plenty of straw for Kialessa to sleep on. Often Kialessa would sit with Piex, and they would discuss home, family or the difference between good and evil in case it helped them get Uncle Tobiuus to set them free.

One evening they sat quietly in their room. Piex was on his bed with his book in his lap, staring at the wall, while Kialessa brushed down his wizard cloak.

'What if he's right?' he said with a sad frown.

'He can't be.'

'But what *is* evil?'

4 At the desk

Kialessa did not know.

Piex thought out loud. 'Maybe evil is all relative. What's evil to one race is good to another. We think it's evil to eat your enemies, but to trolls it's a great honour. So if there's no absolute–'

'But there is absolute evil in this world. You saw it in

 By Dr Joseph Ireland "Dr Joe"

your uncle's left hand. It was the suffering–'

'I know, but isn't suffering sometimes necessary? Don't women suffer giving birth, and that brings out a new life, which surely is good.'

'Then suffering, itself, cannot be evil,' Kialessa agreed. 'So we're left where we started. How do you define evil? I think this is the hardest riddle I've ever heard.'

Piex groaned and nodded, and went back to brooding.

'At least we can all agree on one thing,' she offered. 'Sometimes it just doesn't matter. Forget about it, for now.'

Piex sighed.

'Answers will come, don't get frustrated and try to force them. Keep asking, but just forget it and focus on something else. Have patience. You don't have to answer every question *today*.'

Piex gave her a thin smile. She knew he had more pressing concerns to fill his mind tonight, like dragon riding. Some of the things Uncle Tobiuus expected were pure drudgery, such as polishing boots and impossible riddles almost no one could solve. Then again, some of the things he expected were once in a lifetime opportunities, things like learning to ride a dragon.

Tobiuus expected that all his apprentices would have nothing less than a dragon for a mount one day. None of those furry, thoughtless posks would do. Oh, no! He himself rode the huge rot dragon, Txlax; though no students were permitted to even *think* of riding that beast.

But Txlax had many offspring, seven of which were strong enough to carry students.

Thus, when the evening of Serrosday came along once more, Piex and all the other students went to the roof of the tower to try their luck at claiming one of the younger dragons to practice riding. They held their breath, keeping well away from the tower's sheer edge, and listened as the first apprentice explained once more the process of attracting a dragon mount. Kialessa could hardly wait, but Piex dragged his feet the whole way.

'Here's how it works,' Dusk said. 'Have your servant stand and offer the dragons pickled rats on a stick. Then, if the dragon likes your offering, it will eat the rat, or the servant.' He laughed.

Soon they were lifting their pickled rats high into the air. They smelled like a disgusting mix of overcooked onions and rubbish bins. The dragons, however, loved it. They were great beasts with wings the size of three men laid head to foot. They had sharp spines, perfect for impaling their foes, and sunken faces that made them look like their heads were skulls painted black. Many of the younger ones, too small to carry a rider, tried to join in too but were chased off by older ones. At least thirty young dragons flew in circles above them, eyeing the rats hungrily.

The servants hustled to offer their rats first, but Dusk had a clear advantage as his automaton's wooden arm reached higher than all the rest. In moments he had

     By Dr Joseph Ireland "Dr Joe"

secured the largest black dragon for his own, and they soared into the sky, much like they did every time.

The rest of the servants jumped up and down in a little group, trying to get their rats noticed. Kialessa thought it was foolish to all pile together, and ran instead to the tower parapets. It was a long way down, but she did not care.

Piex would love to ride a dragon, she thought. She promised herself that Piex would get to ride a dragon today.

She hopped and skipped from the stones, and some of the other servants began to watch her. Perhaps they thought she had an idea? Or perhaps they thought that she was insane.

Then the group fell silent.

A deep, rhythmic beating sounded behind Kialessa. She turned around, not daring to breathe.

It was a dragon, less than her arms reach away.

With a shout of surprise she fell backwards off the parapet and onto the stone floor below. The dragon alighted where she had been standing and looked at her in curiosity and amusement.

It was not like the other dragons she had seen. Not like them at all. It was swamp black, but it had many glistening scales, like moonlight dancing on a breeze-touched lake. There were bright silver highlights along the tips of the long frill that went from head to tail, the leading edge of its wings, and its razor-sharp claws. Its head was broader too, and not sunken like the pure rot dragons. Gentle tentacles covered her lower jaw, making her look wise. On her head two twisting, dark antlers lay, and between them the illusion of a darkened moon shone. The dragon was large, not half as large as Txlax, but almost equal in size to the largest black.

'What are you?' it hissed in amusement, speaking Emerellian.

'I'm Kialessa,' she stuttered.

'I didn't ask you your name!' it hissed in an impatient tone.

Kialessa stood up. Her name was important. 'If you please, good dragon,' she apologised. 'But my name is Kialessa, and I am a tae'anaryn.'

The dragon stared at her, eye to eye. 'You do not fear the ledge?'

'No,' Kialessa said, although she was not keen on it either.

'These apprentices disgust me,' it said. 'They fear the air. They fear to fall. They clutch on so much it exhausts them and they are glad to reach the ground again.'

'My master is part dragon. He will not fear the air,' Kialessa said.

'Then you are not a wizard?' the dragon said in surprise.

'No.'

'But you do not fear the air?'

Kialessa thought about that. She was not afraid of the

air, or of riding a dragon. With rising excitement she realised there was nothing more in all the world that she'd like right now than to fly through the air on a dragon.

Piex could wait.

'Not one bit!' she said boldly.

'Then ride with me,' the dragon roared and slid underneath her.

Kialessa shrieked in excitement and fear as the dragon leapt up on the parapets again and began to run, picking up speed.

'Get out of my way,' it shouted to the goblin servants, knocking their rat laden sticks to the ground. They scurried and ducked for their lives.

A goblin wizard protested. 'She's not a wizard!'

One dark look from the dragon silenced him. With a mighty leap, the dragon spread its wings and began to fly.

For the first time she could remember, Kialessa was no longer touching the ground. There was nothing to save her from death but the powerful, steady wing beats of a dragon. She was too excited to be afraid, and so screamed in joy. The dragon responded with a mighty screech of its own. The wind ripped past her face and through her hair faster than she'd ever known, and she was far, far away from Tobiuus's tower in a matter of moments.

'Faster, faster,' she urged the dragon.

It responded in delight. Surging forward, it went into a sudden downwards curve, the wind almost tearing Kialessa from the dragon's back. It whipped around the entire tower in a matter of instants and shot high into the air again, covering the moon with its mighty wings. Then it levelled out, and rested with steady wing beats against the air as it circled the tower.

'That was amazing!' Kialessa said.

'Indeed, you ride well,' the dragon replied.

'What is your name?'

The dragon gave a soft growl. 'A dragon's name is a sacred thing, the archmage forbids me share it. But I do not care. Can you be trusted with a secret?'

Kialessa hesitated. *How good is a secret when an archmage can control my mind?* But she would keep this dragon's secret, even if it cost her mind. 'I can.'

'In Dragonspeech my name is *Eclipsatur Luna sub Bruma.* It refers to the eclipsed moon of the winter solstice.' The dragon sighed. It seemed a great weight had been lifted off her shoulders, as if she had been keeping this name a secret for a long time.

'Names are important, aren't they?' Kialessa said.

'They are.'

'But … I can call you Eclipse?'

The dragon nodded, and seemed to smile. 'That would be suitable.'

They rode in amicable silence for a moment. Kialessa looked at the mighty wings, pushing huge torrents of the unseen air downwards in order to keep them aloft. Surely there was nothing more powerful than a dragon?

 By Dr Joseph Ireland "Dr Joe"

5 Dragon riding

'But why do dragons want a rider?' Kialessa wondered suddenly.

'Few do.' Eclipse replied, 'but in battle our heads and necks are the least protected part of our body. A rider can increase our safety, if they can hold on, that is. Your hands are strong, little one. I do not fear to lose you.'

Kialessa held on tight, hugging the dragon. They rode along in silence a moment more.

'You're not like the rot dragons, are you?'

The creature huffed. 'I am not. My mother was a rare

moon dragon, that much I know. But where she is now, I am not told. I heard she abandoned me before I hatched.'

'That's sad,' Kialessa said.

'It does not matter. Tobiuus and my father raise me harshly, but well.'

'So did mine, I guess.' Kialessa told Eclipse. Though somehow she doubted her upbringing was anything like the dragon's. Kialessa's mother was very selfish and demanding. She hardly ever allowed her out of the kitchen in the inn, but that was probably for the best since most people hated the sight of her. They would sneer or laugh, or sometimes even threaten her just for crossing their path. Her father, the barkeep, was the greatest kindness in her world, when he wasn't too drunk to stand up. But at least she knew she was loved; from the things they said and did. That could have never been as bad as being raised by a murderous dragon and evil, twisted archmage.

'Tobiuus is evil,' Kialessa affirmed.

'Evil? Do you know what that means?'

Kialessa sat in silence. Tobiuus insisted that he was both good and evil, but Kialessa could not bring herself to believe he was anything but bad. She was beginning to think that he had become so evil he couldn't tell anymore. 'I don't know what evil is, but I know Tobiuus is evil.'

Eclipse scoffed at her. 'I do not think so. I have seen how my father hunts for sport, killing the creatures that stray into his swamp. He enjoys causing suffering. He, I think, is evil.'

'So you think causing suffering is evil?'

'I cannot say, because to pull a splinter is painful, but surely to leave it in would be the greater evil.'

So, Eclipse was a philosopher too.

'Well, there's suffering that's necessary, and suffering that's not. Perhaps that's where the line is drawn between what is good and what is evil?' Kialessa suggested. 'Evil is causing unnecessary suffering.'

Eclipse pondered this a moment. 'Surely deliberately causing unnecessary suffering is an evil thing, but there are many more evils in this world. Some evils, such as the goblins who become slothful, claim not to be suffering. They seem to quite enjoy it.'

'Hmmm,' said Kialessa. 'Some of the goblins are very lazy, and it means the others do have to work harder. Maybe they are causing *others* to suffer?'

'Hrumph,' Eclipse disagreed. 'And at what point does suffering become unnecessary? Say you captured an enemy and they had information you needed. Would it not be prudent to force that information from them? To cause them to suffer, so that you could be safe?'

'No, that would be evil,' Kialessa said.

'I think not.'

'Why?'

'Because there is no absolute evil, or so my father teaches me. Do you know what it means to be good?' Eclipse laughed. 'Goodness and evil are two sides of the same coin. There is no goodness, only what you prefer.'

'I once was told that goodness is to do to others what you would have done to you, in their place. If you were captured, and someone wanted information from you, how would you *want*, not expect, to be treated?'

Eclipse was silent for a moment. 'I don't think I'd let myself be captured,' she concluded with confidence.

Kialessa continued. 'I wouldn't want to be forced to give someone what they wanted, if it was precious to me. Not ever. Even if it gave them great power, even if they said it was to save lives. Besides, if it was for the best, I'd give it away freely. I would not have to be imprisoned to give it away.'

Eclipse laughed. 'Perhaps you are too weak, then? Your enemies will prosper and you will go without. In the end, you may fall, and your high ideals of goodness will be lost to the world.'

Kialessa looked out at the moon, a silver crescent waxing silently in the nighttime sky. 'I think you underestimate the power of goodness.'

Eclipse chuckled. 'I have seen Tobiuus do many great acts of goodness. He saved the nearby goblin villages from starvation. He has crafted weapons of light to protect a king in a faraway land. He has saved much research from forgotten people across the world. Will you still say he is wholly evil?'

Kialessa did not know what to say. 'A few good deeds don't cover up a lifetime of evil. He is evil, or what he's doing is.'

'What, training your wizard? I would think that counts as good.'

'We are not here by choice.'

'Oh. Then you are prisoners too.'

'What do you mean?'

Eclipse was silent for a moment. 'He does not allow me to leave. One day, he intends for me to replace my father,' she said in cold spite. 'My father is such a fool; he has no idea. But I do not hold out much hope for him once I am of age. The archmage keeps me on a diet of rare herbs that increases my growth. I suppose a child of a moon dragon and a rot dragon is more to his taste than a simple rot dragon. Once I am large enough for an adult human to ride, he will dispense with my father permanently.'

Kialessa was silent. How could Eclipse not see that Tobiuus was being evil? He had fallen from the path of goodness a long time ago, and the evil had made him blind to his fall. Now he was trying to convince this dragon too.

At just that moment, a mighty ball of fire lit the night sky near the tower.

'Time to return,' Eclipse said, turning without hesitation. 'There will likely be punishment for my failure to take a wizard today.'

But it sounded like she was smiling.

'You like disobeying him, don't you?' Kialessa said as they whirled back towards the tower.

Eclipse laughed a gentle laugh. 'When you need me again, call my name softly. I will hear.'

They landed in silence. Indeed, Tobiuus was angry. Txlax struck his daughter at Tobiuus's command, but there was no further rebuke for her. Kialessa copped another curse that made her feet sting like she was stepping on broken glass every time she took a step for the next day, but she knew its effects would not last forever. Not nearly as long as the memory of making a new friend, and of riding a mighty dragon through the moonlit sky beside an evil wizard's tower.

       By Dr Joseph Ireland "Dr Joe"

The test

Does wisdom teach you? Do you steal treasures from the sacred past? Or let them lie, gaining the greater truth?
– Nemon, 3rd Sage of Lumos, keeper of times.

Myaday of the next week they waited in the darkness with sweaty palms.

'Why does he make us do this?' Kialessa asked.

'It's "real life practice".' Piex mocked his own words, words spoken at the college they'd almost forgotten by now. 'He thinks it teaches us, prepares us for the times when we will plunder dungeons in search of ancient secrets. Secrets he, no doubt, expects us to bring to him.'

Piex had risen to become the fifth apprentice, so they were the fifth to take the test. The other apprentices and their servants had braved the illusionary dungeon, and all had fled injured and terrified. All except Dusk, who laughed as the others failed repeatedly. The other three had terrible burns and cuts. One was trying to wash off flesh eating liquid. Kialessa told herself again and again that it was only an illusion, that they weren't in any real danger. That the sensation of burning or being eaten alive would wear off in a few moments. But it would still hurt. It was real pain, as Tobiuus said when he had lectured them in an almost apologetic manner on the need to face as realistic a challenge as possible in order to bring out their best. Terrible things had happened to the others and their goblin servants. It was not like King Dunnkan's security-rich and entertainment-high training grounds. Not like them at all.

Kialessa thought Tobiuus must enjoy seeing their fear.

'We're ready,' Piex announced.

The lights went on and a jungle with rich foliage appeared from the air around them. They found themselves in a clearing. In front of them a small pyramid rose, covered heavily by vines. The air was thick, humid and hot, even though the sun could not be seen through the thick canopy of the jungle.

'Looks like a forgotten jungle of the archipelago,' Piex muttered.

'Very lifelike,' Kialessa mused in wonder.

'He's probably been here before. This is likely an enhancement based on an experience he's actually had, or the collusion of several altogether. Watch your step.'

They had only moved a pace or two before some leaves begun rustling from behind the pyramid. Then there was a terrific hoot – a shuddering, inhuman sound that cut through the thick forest air like a knife. From around the pyramid, dark grey monkeys with huge canine teeth began to prowl, laughing and staring at them with red, inhuman eyes. They beat the ground with their fists in warning.

'Baboons,' Piex stalled.

'What do we do?'

'Fight them off, I guess.'

'Fight? Not very wizardly of him, is it?'

'That's why he likes us to bring along servants.'

She looked at Piex and hoped he was joking. So that was the other reason Tobiuus thought wizards needed servants, apart from having an audience. Wizards needed servants to put themselves in danger for them.

The baboons were closing in, defending their territory.

'Maybe we can drive them off?' She unhooked her whip and cracked it high above their heads. They backed off for a moment, but the angry sound seemed to provoke them further. She swapped it for the steel bow Tobiuus had loaned her. Again, the baboons approached.

'Let me try. *Somno Lumina*,' he unleashed his favourite spell, and an explosion of starlights sprang from his outstretched hand. Five of the baboons fell over, unconscious. The remaining one, the largest one, fled as soon as an arrow imbedded itself in the ground in front of it. It seemed to know there were none to stand by it in a fight.

'I just love that enchantment,' Kialessa smiled as they ran. 'Practical *and* gorgeous!'

They raced to the pyramid, trying to get it open before the baboons awoke. In front of the pyramid a brief flight of stairs ran down to a stone door, but Kialessa stopped short once she noticed the strange grooves that ran along the low side walls.

'Hold it, Piex. Look at this.' She tossed a rock down first, and as soon as it hit the second stair, two armed clubs with iron spikes swung outwards, sweeping right across the step and then clicked back into the groves.

'That explains the leg wounds on the others,' he muttered. 'How do we get past it?'

One at a time, she tested it by throwing three more rocks down the stairs. 'Just don't step on the second stair.' She hopped down.

Piex was more wary, but made his way to her side.

'Now, how do we get in the pyramid?' she asked.

Piex pondered the door. 'There appear to be three buttons here and they have symbols. Look, I think they are constellations. The Cross and the Questioner, except it contains a few more stars than our constellation does.'

'Almost could be a scorpion tail. Eh?'

'That's … creative. Anyway, this third one is completely blank, just a few stars on the outside.'

'So which button is it?'

'How am I to know?'

One of the baboons began to stir.

Suddenly Kialessa shouted, 'Here!' She began rubbing the weeds away from the just above the door. Some things were written there in a strange language she did not know.

'I think it's Dragonspeech,' Piex said, getting exited. 'Yes, it is Dragonspeech!'

The baboon stood and stumbled around sleepily, so Kialessa had no time to ask him what he meant and shoved him over to read it.

'I think it says something like, "sacred site dedicated to the wizard Broack, servant of the … unmoving … constellation. Let his sisters and brothers enter openly, I mean, freely".'

'Right,' said Kialessa, eyeing the baboons as they stirred. The trap might slow them, but no doubt the baboons could jump too. 'So which is the unmoving constellation? It's not the last one. It's not even a constellation.'

'Actually,' Piex pondered, thinking so deeply about the puzzle it was as if he'd forgotten entirely about the baboons and their sharp teeth. 'I think it might be. The Cross and the Questioner are both stars of the southern hemisphere where we dwell. Like all constellations, they move during the night at the same rate as the sun does during the day.'

'They do?' Kialessa had never noticed the stars doing that.

'They do. But there are two locations of the night sky where -'

'Can we get to the point?' Kialessa hurried him along.

'Where the stars do not move: The celestial poles. All other stars move around those points. The north celestial pole has a star, called the Ice Queen's Palace. But the south pole has no stars. It is blank.'

'So the family of the wizard Broack, would serve the unmoving … oh, for the love of the Patient!' she said, and threw her fist against the third button just as the baboons stumble about and hooted again.

The door slid upwards and they leapt inside. The baboons were still scrambling about, bleary eyed, as Kialessa and Piex hurried to find the closing mechanism, and not a moment too soon. The baboons' screeching howls echoed painfully in the tiny room as the door slid closed.

'I hope we don't have to fight our way out,' Kialessa said.

Piex used a common light spell to illuminate the room they were in; a little ball of glowing yellow light floating around in the air.

It was a simple temple built for tall adults. It was preserved by magic, yet Kialessa could feel the weight of a million years of silence. In the centre of the room was a long sarcophagus, unimaginably old, but the stone lid was still intact after all that time. Along the walls a dim mosaic was still visible.

Carefully, they made their way along the room. It did not appear to have more traps, but there was no way out. She looked everywhere for hidden doors or boxes, until at last they faced the inevitable.

'We'll have to open the sarcophagus,' Piex said.

Kialessa curled up her nose. 'Are you sure?'

'Yep, it's just what Uncle Tobiuus would expect.'

'But,' she hesitated, 'isn't that where someone's dead body is lying? I don't want to be a grave robber.'

'I know,' Piex agreed. 'Try to think of it … as research.'

'Research?'

'Yeah, this is the body of a long dead wizard from a long dead civilisation from which we can learn many great things. We can also preserve their treasures properly in museums where they are defended well and can be appreciated and studied by wizards from all over the world.'

Clearly he'd given this some previous thought.

'I still think it's wrong. Who gives us permission to disturb his grave?'

'Well, if we were still in the High Kingdom we could get permission from the hero's guild or archaeological society. They pay well too, I hear.'

The thought that they would get permission, not payment, cheered her up. 'And since we're in an illusion created by your uncle we can assume that we have already gotten the archaeological licence through honest means.'

Piex was silent. 'But you're a tae'anaryn.'

Clearly he was thinking that breaking laws wasn't hard for a tae'anaryn. Well, it was! Not counting when they had broken into Master De'Feur's study earlier that year, but that was for a good cause!

'Being a tae'anaryn doesn't automatically make me dishonest.'

'Sorry, you're right. Yes, we've gone to the archaeologist's guild–'

'And *now* we're going to take the lid off this coffin.'

He rolled his eyes. They checked for possible traps, and pushing together, heaved the heavy stone lid off the stone box.

Inside it was all dust and some rubble.

'Thieves have been here already,' he said.

'Why would they put the lid back on?'

'Maybe it magicked itself back?'

They looked at the dusty, empty box.

'Well, go on, have a good look,' he said.

'But …' she began, but she wasn't going to argue with her wizard on a day that Tobiuus might be looking. And if there was a trap, only she was quick enough to avoid it.

She jumped inside and felt around, but inside there was nothing. Even the bones had turned to dust.

'Nothing but a few pebbles, some scraps of metal, and some little tiles,' she said, holding one up.

         By Dr Joseph Ireland "Dr Joe"

'It has the number four on it in Dragonspeech.'

For a moment Kialessa just look at him, till he seemed to realise this might be a clue. She smiled at him, and scurried around the inside of the box, collecting eight more tiles. As she did, Piex lined them up in order. Numbers one through nine.

'Look,' Kialessa said in astonishment. 'There's a grid here the right size for the tiles to fit in!'

'Wait, don't!' Piex said. 'It might be dangerous to get them in the wrong order.'

'Well,' she said, getting out again, 'what order do they go in this grid?'

'There must be a pattern, an organisation. Some form of meaning,' Piex mused, looking over the riddle, getting lost again in his excitement to meet a new challenge.

'Here,' she said again. 'There's another number just below the grid. See this? What is it?'

'It's fifteen, going by the patterns of the other numbers. They appear to have a base ten number system.'

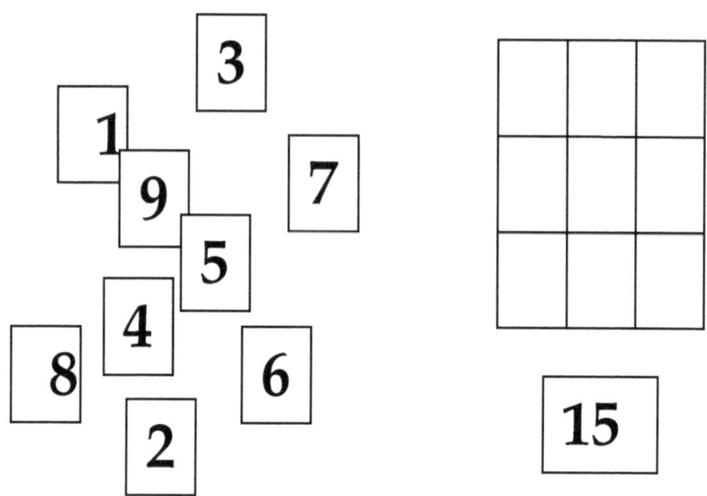

'Base ten?' Kialessa asked.

'Yeah, numbers repeating every ten digits, with the position of the number relative to the others denoting a tenfold value – one, ten, one hundred, and so forth.'

'What?'

'Don't worry about it.' He began arranging the numbers in a practice grid, trying to make each line add up to fifteen, but after five moments he began to wear out.

'It's terrible,' he moaned. 'Without knowing the position of at least one number it's very difficult to arrange the rest. I can get all the horizontal lines to equal fifteen, but the vertical ones do not. Somehow, I do not think this is sufficient.'

Kialessa waited.

'There must be a further clue in the room somewhere,' he said.

They began to look around again and it was only a moment before Kialessa found another number cut into the floor. It was so faded, if she hadn't seen the ones in the sarcophagus, she would not have noticed it. Soon they found another and another.

'They're forming a pattern,' she said. 'A straight line, crossing this room. There's the one at the door, and nine at the opposite wall, and all the numbers move in towards the centre. But where is the number five?'

They couldn't see it anywhere.

'I get it!' Piex announced. 'It's five, five is in the centre. See, going from one door to the wall the number five would appear right in the centre of this grid. You did it, Kialessa. We've got it!'

Before she could stop him, he'd plonked the number five tile right in the middle. Nothing happened.

'Let's get the other numbers right before we move on,' she said. He replied thankfully, realising too late that his enthusiasm could have endangered them both.

'Five, now. Five is in the middle.'

'And everything else revolves around that,' Kialessa said.

'Just like the south celestial pole!'

Whoever had built the tomb had a pattern here, always placing things in the middle.

Soon Piex had the other tiles arranged in his practice grid so that they all added to fifteen, even diagonally. 'Still, I can rotate the figure into at least four configurations, so I'm not sure which number to put in the corner.'

'Maybe there are more clues?'

'Or maybe not. I myself understand magic well enough to make a similar cipher function in four correct combinations. Or perhaps we can safely assume they would place number one in the centre top, assuming their written language moved top to bottom as ours does. I think we can risk it.' He said stood back, waiting for her to do it.

She rolled her eyes. What a lazy wizard! Or perhaps there was sense in what he was doing, since she had much better reactions than he did. She put the pieces into the grid inside the sarcophagus, one at a time, from one to nine. As soon as she'd finished the tiles clicked downwards in what had appeared to be solid stone.

6	1	8
7	5	3
2	9	4

'Uh, oh,' she said, and leapt out of the sarcophagus.

The room then began to descend downwards like a lift. The walls sloped away from them as they descended, and it became apparent that they were standing in a far larger pyramid than she had originally thought. It was huge and stretched out into the darkness almost to the limit of the light. Shadows seemed to scurry and flicker in the darkness, and there, just at the edge of the light, dozens of corridors continued into the darkness. The lift stopped far below the entry way in the enormous pyramid, and the place where they stood was surrounded by dark, silent water.

'Serendipitous,' Piex whispered in awe. 'We have done well.'

They stood there in silence for a moment.

'Hey,' Piex suddenly blurted out, 'what if there is no good or evil; only obedience. The gods strive to bring order and impose law to do so, punishing those who disobey. In their order, growth is possible, and the weak have a greater chance to survive. Outside, chaos rules. Therefore, there is no evil, only disobedience to the laws the order the gods impose.'

'What do you mean?' She wondered why on earth he'd think of this right now.

'If the purpose of being is to grow and develop, than anything that opposes that is evil. Chaos, therefore, is evil. And the order that brings about civilisation is good.'

'Where did that come from?'

'I don't know.'

Kialessa thought, 'But sometimes isn't a little chaos is a good thing? I mean, history is full of heroes who did the right thing in spite of the evil laws of gods and kings.'

'Hmmm.' He looked out at the darkness. 'So perhaps chaos and law are not enough to define good and evil either …'

They pondered in silence for a moment.

'What I don't get,' Kialessa said, 'is why wizards go to all this trouble to make a tomb, and then fill it with puzzles so that anyone can break in and help themselves to their treasures? Why not just use a lock?'

'Locks can be picked or opened magically with simple spells,' Piex explained. 'Tombs enspelled with riddles like this are much harder to break into, and it makes the doors almost unbreakable.'

'Oh, I see. Magic is kind of weird like that isn't it? Besides, this guy probably had descendants or students for many generations coming to speak to his spirit or to pay their respects. Remember, the "sisters and brothers" were welcome. They would have known the answers.'

'Good point,' Piex said. 'And the unwelcomed would have been killed by now. Many ancient cultures believed their dead needed their treasures from life to help them in the next world. Thieves would break in and steal those treasures, if they could, instead of treating them like important historical artefacts. So traps and puzzles like these were set to discourage or kill intruders.'

'What if the dead really did need their treasures?' She asked.

'I suppose that is possible …'

Kialessa stepped forward to study the water that

surrounded their small platform.

'Don't touch it!' Piex said, and bent down to sniff it. 'Just what I thought. It's highly caustic. The opposite to acid and just as dangerous. It would sting painfully, and if you don't wash it off immediately, it will eat your flesh. You'd be gone in less than a day, maybe less. Much less if it's magically enhanced.'

She shrank back from the water.

Wizards are very useful, at times, she thought.

'So, where to now?' Kialessa asked.

'I have no idea.'

Test continues

There are many who would try and teach you what evil is, and many other things. I think you should listen to them all, and search for yourself the truth in all their contradicting words. Great words matter, but it is what you believe that will guide your own actions.

– Broak, the pre-ancient.

They stood at the bottom of an enormous, dark, pyramid shaped cavern. There were many exists, but their small island, only large enough for them and an empty sarcophagus, was surrounded by flesh eating water.

'There must be a safe way to cross,' she said. 'But even if we did, how would we know which corridor to take?'

'I don't know. There's got to be a clue somewhere.'

'But how can we get there through this toxic water?'

'There might be stones in the water.' Piex suggested, but they could find none. 'Or maybe it is as I feared, the magic might carry you across the water, but only if you're walking in the right direction.'

'And if you're wrong?'

Suddenly, Piex's light went out.

'Oh, yeah, forgot about that,' he admitted.

'Do you have another one?'

'Umm well, sorry. I've run out of ingredients, and I prepared all my other light spells on scrolls, so I can't actually read them now.'

'What!'

'Sorry. I was supposed to be timing the spell.'

'Oh, great! Can't you read in the dark?'

'No.'

They thought in silence. Piex got his scroll out anyway.

'Wait a moment, I do see something!' he said. 'Look up on the roof!'

Sure enough, tiny pin pricks of light covered the roof of the pyramid.

'Holes? Do you think it might cave in?' Kia asked.

'No, I think they're magical lights. Look, they're constellations, but a little different from the ones we know. See, the arms of the cross are tilted, and look.' He continued to point out subtle differences. 'I wonder why that would be, when the stars are fixed and immovable?'

'No they're not, you said they're not.'

'Oh, yes, no, that's because we're on a world that turns.'

'We are?' She'd never heard that.

'That's sagemaster Priax's second postulate. It was originally considered heresy, but it does simplify calculating the movement of the five planets in the night sky,' and on and on he went.

'So,' she finally interrupted. 'Which way's out?'

'I don't know.'

'I think it's obvious. Which constellation did they revere the most?'

'The one that didn't move!' he said, understanding.

She made him hold her tail as she walked underneath the dark patch of sky, though he was unsure at first. She insisted that if she fell into the water, he could use it to pull her out, but in reality she just wanted to make sure he followed her in the near pitch darkness. He seemed to be much worse than her at seeing his way in the darkness. As they walked towards the corridor underneath the gap in the sky that represented the south celestial pole, stones rose up to help them across the water.

They were both grateful to feel the normal earth beneath their feet again. The corridor beyond was short, but Piex was still worried about the darkness.

After a brief walk they came to another sarcophagus, far more ornate than the last one. The room itself was covered in statues and paintings of considerable value. But Kialessa seemed to be the only one who could

        By Dr Joseph Ireland "Dr Joe"

appreciate it in the dimly lit cave. She was about to check for traps, but the moment they stepped into the room two torches burst magically to life.

'This must be his real tomb,' Piex said, seeing it all for the first time.

'It won't be,' Kia stated, 'just another decoy.'

'How can you tell?'

'It's not in the centre. A wizard like this would not hide his personal treasures for the afterlife in a coffin by the wall.'

'Good point. But maybe that's just what he *expected* us to think?'

'Look, I see a new puzzle already.'

At the far wall, underneath another motif of the unmoving constellation, a dark and dusty object sat on a plate. Underneath the dust was a brightly coloured cube, each face a different colour. Each colour was divided into nine sections.

'Another puzzle?' Kia asked.

'I guess so.'

'Do we touch it?'

They both stood there, looking.

'I'd better.' Piex said. 'It might adhere to the person who touches it.' The moment his finger touched the cube, it twisted and turned itself around until all the colours were mixed up in random patterns across the cube. They'd never seen anything like this strange, foreign object.

6 The curious device neither of them had ever seen before...

'Oh,' Kialessa said.

'Seems pretty simple.' He picked it up off the floor.

But it was not. Five moments went by, then more. He was not getting any closer to completing the puzzle. Every time he turned one colour, it shifted the arrangement of the entire cube.

'Argh. This is frustrating. If I had a few days, sure, but this is crazy!'

'Wizards,' Kialessa muttered.

'There has to be some kind of pattern to it, or short cut. There must be a clue around here somewhere.'

But instead of searching around, Kialessa searched her memory. The whole crypt was about the "unmoving constellation" that was in the centre.

The centre! she thought.

Looking at the strange cube, Kialessa realised that the one colour on each side that Piex couldn't move were the colours in the centre of each face. That must be the colour that determined what all other colours should be. As soon

        By Dr Joseph Ireland "Dr Joe"

as she told Piex, it was a matter of twenty or so moments before he'd sorted it out. Being as careful as he could, he replaced the completed cube back on the plate.

'I enjoyed that challenge.' He smiled.

For an instant, nothing happened. Then there was a crack of thunder followed by the grinding of mighty stone. The room flooded with intense light as the instant sarcophagus slid to one side to reveal a well-lit ramp leading down into the ground, back in the direction they'd come.

'In other words,' Kialessa said, 'back towards the centre.'

Piex smiled.

They walked down with care. The walls were soft blue, glowing gently and perfectly flat. It was unlike any architecture she'd ever seen. The walls were lit every three strides or so with a brightly glowing orb.

'That'd make nice treasure,' Kialessa said.

'They might, or they might trigger another trap, and the whole dungeon might collapse. If this is his real burial place and we set it off that's just what might happen. We'd better be careful from here.'

'And we weren't before?' Kialessa muttered.

They soon came to a door that opened without a sound to reveal a simple crypt, preserved without flaw so that it looked like it was built yesterday. Gentle pictures of a great wizard's life ringed the walls and soft music played. Somehow, in spite of the all the years, the air was cool and clear. Around the walls several benches lay where people could sit, and the far wall was a collection of drawers and shelves all the way to the roof. The sarcophagus that was in the centre of the room was topped with glass.

'I dare you to look,' Kialessa teased.

Without hesitation, and to Kialessa's complete surprise, Piex walked straight up to it. 'If it is a test of wisdom, I'm likely to fare better,' he said, more practical than arrogant. When there appeared to be no further tests or traps to pass, Kialessa came up to watch too.

Inside was a perfectly preserved man in strange clothes. He had dark trousers and a dark cloak that was short, almost like a jacket. The only colour he wore was a strange strip of fabric around his neck that lay down his chest.

'A badge of office?' Kialessa said.

Piex shrugged.

He wore golden rings and strange footwear. They were shoes, but were black and apparently unsown in any way.

Piex read the name plaque, written in Dragonspeech. 'Here lies the wizard Broack, whose cutting-edge research has allowed humanity to reach beyond the stars and peer into the material dimensions of air and earth. Born 2295 AD – Died 2504 AD. A life to, um … rejoice.'

'What do you suppose it all means?' Kialessa said.

'Sounds like he might have generated dimensional

portal spells for his people that have allowed them to visit the elemental planes of air and earth. I don't know why they don't mention the other elemental planes. It's the same spell. And look at this. He lived for almost three hundred years, a curiously long life for the average human. He does look human, doesn't he?'

'Yes, he does. He is very well preserved. Do you know what AD stands for?'

'No idea. Maybe someone at the archaeologists' guild has some idea. The pyramid looks old.'

'Older than our ancestors?'

'Thousands of years older. Maybe even older than the Ancients. This is a really important find,' he said sadly. 'If there are others of these in the area it would mean a lifetime of research opportunities.'

'What's so sad about that?'

'Tobiuus probably destroyed it after he'd plundered all the treasure, wanting to keep it all to himself.'

'Don't say that so loud,' she whispered. They were in an illusion, and surely Tobiuus was listening to every word they said.

'We'd better check the room out for magical items. It's what Tobiuus would expect. I hope we don't have to disturb the spirit of the dead by opening that sarcophagus.'

Suddenly, there was a jolt and the whole air shimmered as if the illusion were struggling to survive. The room was touched by a chill, and the air smelt different. The lights dimmed for a moment, and a ghostly form began to materialise above the sarcophagus.

They flung themselves against the back wall and Kialessa stifled a scream.

'How long has it been?' The ghost whispered. He looked and dressed, in every way, like the wizard in the tomb.

Kialessa was too frightened to move, even if it was an illusion.

'I see you there, children. Talk to me,' he said, his voice kind now. 'How long has it been? I have long moved on, but your presence has reawakened me, or a part of me, it seems.'

Kialessa shoved Piex forward.

He trembled, but stood forward with courage. 'Great wizard Broack, we are humble seekers of knowledge. Please, will you share what you know?'

'Know!' the wizard's spirit became sorrowful, then angry. 'Have you lived to see the fall of your people? A hundred billion souls all too desperate to survive? You cannot begin to understand what I *know*. I died over a thousand years before my people's demise, but a part of my spirit has lived on through the science of wizardry in this chamber, counselling them, watching them grow. They became a *mighty* people. Then many of them became arrogant, too full of their own council to hear wisdom any longer. When the time came for them to move on I watched the fall of those who insisted on staying. They lost the light of hope, of art, of prayer. They became increasingly violent and evil until war overtook them all. Then there was no place left for them. Now they are all gone, and I fear for the world.'

'But we are here,' Piex said.

The wizard smiled; his voice now soft once more. 'Indeed you are, and perhaps that is good for the world. That means things have changed, changed from what it once was … too wise to listen to council anymore.'

'Is that why they died?'

'Not all died, but all are gone. And even I am only a shadow, a part of a soul that has been permitted to remain, to warn the next ones.'

'Who were your people, mighty wizard? Are you the Ancients of *Civit Aurea* whose mighty civilisation spread throughout the land thousands of years ago?'

He seemed to think about this for a bit. 'Oh, we are from much, much further back. I sense a very, very long time has been since our two peoples spoke. Have you no record of us? Have you no name for us? I could tell you how long it has been if you had a name for us.'

But they did not.

Broack thought some more, then continued. 'We are the people who came *before* the people. There was no land on this world we did not touch, no star in the heavens we did not visit. We are and will always be the greatest civilisation to ever be born on this great world.' He grew sad again. 'We are those who stopped the moon.'

'The moon was not once fixed in the sky?' Piex asked with wonder.

'Indeed, it used to cross the sky every twenty-five hours or so, just as the sun still does today. But during the great wars that ended, they decided it was the cause of all their woes. And so they stopped the moon, but it brought them no peace.'

'That's wizardry of unimaginable power,' Piex marvelled.

'Indeed it was,' Broack said, his voice soft.

'You know, you're a remarkably knowledgeable and friendly illusion.' Piex said, probably trying to compliment both Broack and Uncle Tobiuus in one.

'Oh,' Broack explained with a wink. 'This stopped being his illusion as soon as I manifested.'

Kialessa gasped.

'Where are we?' Piex said, his voice choked with fear.

'With me,' Broack replied.

Piex turned pale.

'But do not fear. When I removed you, I also created an illusion: one of you searching around for treasures. Be sure not to tell *him*.' He winked again. 'I have been granted this privilege to tell you a mystery, and to show that the wisdom of goodness is always greater than the cunning of evil. I know you are prisoners and that you long to escape. I have been permitted to show you how.'

'Really? Where are we?' Piex said again. It was as if he was more interested in what the wizard Broack had done than that he had just told them he knew how to escape.

'*When*, not *where*, is the more appropriate question. But your people only seem to have just begun to uncover the secrets of time and energy, of thought and matter. Do they even know what they do when they create an "illusion"?' He laughed to himself. 'But I boast. I have a message for you, children. A riddle, before you must leave. Would you like to hear it now?'

'Yes please.'

The wizard spoke:

'Under the tower, silver and black,
A prisoner waits, her freedoms lack.
A prisoner bold and kind and true,
Protect her heart from darkness new.
The other chained in towers tall,
Bitter, vengeful, darkness fall.
Two prisoners, but one key,
Both are trapped, both to free.
Answers simple; for you see,
The one's chain, the other's key.
When once you know, as so one should,
Knowing evil, yet choosing good.'

'So that's your message then?' Kialessa said.

'Indeed it is. I'm glad to have shared it with you,' the wizard's spirit said.

'Thank you, Broack.' Piex bowed low.

They all stood looking at each other for a moment.

'Don't you have to leave after you've delivered your message?' Piex asked.

'Nope,' Broack replied, the hint of laughter in his voice, 'I can keep this up all day. I mean, it's been countless years since I last had a good chat to mortals and I'm having a great time. So what are they teaching you young ones at college now?'

Kialessa was a bit surprised. 'Isn't it, "I have but a short time among your kind"?' Kialessa quoted a story she'd once heard.

'Ahh, young ones, how much I could teach you, being where I am now! But you would not understand any of it. So I and the others must wait until you *show* you are ready, and help you in your efforts, and protect you, and forgive your many failures. Forgiving, even as I was forgiven for my many failures.' He sighed with memories unshared. 'Anyway, your manner of dress is strange. Is *that* what they put wizards in nowadays?' he asked, pretending to be indignant, and they laughed.

They talked a good half hour, chatting away, but he would tell them little more about his people. He was interested in hearing about their friends, their family and their college. He wasn't at all surprised or bothered about Kialessa being a tae'anaryn. They told him all about their abduction, and he was interested to learn about how they hoped to escape, offering kind suggestions and friendly advice. He told them to make the most of their current situation, but indicated that the riddle held the key to their escape.

It felt good to talk to someone who listened.

Piex, naturally, took the opportunity to ask the question that was plaguing him the most. 'What, good wizard Broack, do you say is the nature of evil?'

He smiled. 'What do you say, good apprentice?'

Piex stumbled for words, but in the end, admitted defeat. 'I'm not sure.'

'There are many who would try and teach you what evil is, and many other things. I think you should listen to them all, and search for yourself the truth in all their contradicting words. Great words matter, but it is what you *believe* that will guide your own actions. What you believe is more important to your life than all the great works of all the great scholars of all time. You must decide for yourself.'

Piex sighed. He appeared to be comforted, though the words didn't seem to be helpful to Kialessa. Perhaps Piex wasn't so worried about getting it "right" now, but about finding his own answer and letting it grow with him.

Then Broack told them it was time for him to leave. He showed them where the magic ring was that Tobiuus expected them to claim. Then, with as warm a handshake as a ghost can give, he bid them both farewell.

The look of envy in the other students' faces when they left the illusion was priceless, and the look of surprise in Dusk's very satisfying. Tobiuus, however, was disappointed that they didn't plunder the whole room while they were down there.

'He didn't need it anymore,' he said.

But they were silent. They knew they had found a far better treasure than golden rings and seamless shoes.

The dungeon & the dragon

'These lies are old, youngling, very, very old. There is power in evil, but it will always lead to suffering and regret in the end. Goodness, properly practiced, will always lead to strength and joy at the last. It really is as simple as that.'

– Norius, Moon dragon, cited by Piex. Castle records 63.2.313 CY

'What do you suppose the riddle means?' Kialessa asked Piex after they'd gotten through the rest of the day and went to their room, the room of the third apprentice.

But Piex held his fingers to his lips to indicate that it was not a safe place to speak. He tried to tell her using a cypher he'd made, but that only made things more confusing. So finally he wrote a brief message on some paper and handed it to her. It only took her five moments to understand; she was getting far better at reading, after all. *Let's look for this prisoner "under the tower". We'll try the secret room you found before, near the kitchen.* When she had read it, he burnt the paper.

An hour later they pressed the door carefully open. Some goblin guards were talking down the corridor, but they left after a few moments.

Kialessa and Piex crept out. They didn't speak as they made their way to a stairwell at the back of the apprentice's dormitories. Down, down they hurried. The stones were cold, and the stairs steep. As luck would have it, none of the goblin servants seemed to be using them at the time. Eventually they came to the bottom of the stairs and entered the storage area.

'I think one of the prisoners is you,' he finally whispered. 'And the other one must be somewhere down here. Let's find her, and "protect her heart from darkness new".'

'Me?' Kialessa asked in surprise. 'What makes you think that? And how will we know when we find the other prisoner?'

'I don't know. I guess it'll be the one that won't eat us if she's supposed to be good, or at least, not "bitter".'

'That's very little comfort,' Kialessa pointed out.

They looked around at the crowded storage room, and it seemed deserted.

'*Aperire*,' she whispered. The stones began to move and shift in their places, though this time she could feel the invisible magic in the words swirl around the room. Soon the stairs extended further.

'What if Dusk is down there?' she said.

'It's a risk, I know.'

They hurried down the steps. The room below was dark and loathsome. Dank water tricking from a sorry puddle to the left as shadows flicked suspiciously from two poorly lit magical torches. A single unattended desk sat to one side, and four thick, reinforced doors were positioned around the room.

'Do you know what this place is?' she asked.

'Tobiuus's dungeon,' Piex replied.

'Do you think the spir –' but Piex's look silenced her. She felt safe, but if their uncle somehow found out about the spirit that had taken them from the illusion, they'd be in terrible trouble. She hoped this was the place the spirit had referred to in its riddle, the place "under the tower", for it certainly was a tower of silver and black. 'Do you think any apprentices ended up here?'

'I don't think so. Tobiuus is a criminal, but he's not *that* wicked. It most likely imprisons some poor beasts for his experiments.'

'But Txlax told me he eats apprentices that fail.'

Piex looked at her, but said nothing. He went to check the papers on the desk. 'Goblin script. This one's probably a record or something. The rest is just scrawling to pass the time, I presume.'

'Why isn't the goblin here now?' she asked.

'No idea.' Piex looked concerned. 'What if they find us?'

'We're just snooping around again.'

'I hate having Tobiuus spells cast at me. If he turns both my feet left again!'

'I know,' Kialessa said. 'I know.'

It had been a rough half season.

They looked at the doors with great care. They all had strange symbols carved on them. Behind one an enormous creature snored, behind another strange scratches and giggles ensued. A third was silent, but they both felt faint as they approached.

The fourth door was completely silent.

'I think I hear something breathing,' Kialessa said.

'I hope it's something good,' Piex said.

'How do we know which door to choose?'

'I have no idea. Which one do you want to try?'

'The fourth. I have no idea why.'

'Go ahead then,' he said.

She walked up to the door.

They removed the heavy iron bar without much effort, but the door itself was locked. Piex's simple opening spell was enough to unlock the door, but still it did not open. Piex cast his simple Inflornium spell, and sure enough, a strange puzzle began to unfold itself from the door. There were nine dots, arranged in three rows of three.

Underneath them was a new riddle:

Four lines I am
Four lines I need
Four lines alone
Or you will bleed.

Your finger the pencil
With which to write
But lift the pencil
And lose your sight.

'Wizard locks,' Kialessa huffed in frustration.

'Precisely. Or maybe he expects disobedient apprentices to break into his dungeon, give the lock a go without thinking about it and go blind from the experience,' Piex muttered.

He knelt down and drew the dots in the dust on the floor, trying to trace out four lines, end to end, without lifting his finger. It only took him a moment to announce it was clearly impossible.

'C'mon Piex, think creatively. Think "outside the square" as they say. Maybe it's a riddle itself, or there's something else about the door –'

'Outside the square!' Piex laughed too loudly. 'Of course, look.' And he drew four lines, without lifting his finger, that went all the way thought each dot by going outside the square that confined them.

Four lines I am
Four lines I need
Four lines alone
Or you will bleed.

Your finger the pencil
With which to write
But don't lift the pencil
Or lose your sight.

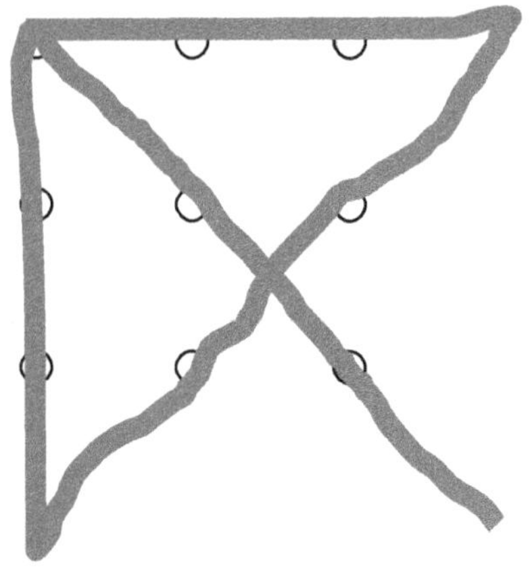

'You're so clever,' he complimented her.

'But you solved the puzzle.' She smiled.

He jumped up to open the door, but then stood back to let her do it; just in case it exploded, or they really were blinded.

How thoughtful, she grumbled. But after she'd pushed on the door, it clicked open without trouble and they hurried inside.

Inside it was dark once again. Something big was sleeping inside, but they shut the door anyway. Hoping the wizard Broack's riddle was right, and that they'd picked the right door, and that there was something "good" in here. Piex used his light spell, and they gasped.

There, glistening in the shadows, was a dragon. Its mud-covered scales hid a gentle silver sheen, and the frills that ran from its face to its tail were limp and weary. One of its mighty antlers was missing, and its claws wasted

        By Dr Joseph Ireland "Dr Joe"

limply in the mud. It had no wings and was long and coiled, like a snake. Clearly it was a mighty sky dragon, one of the good dragons.

'A moon dragon,' Piex whispered, his voice soft and reverent.

It was now that Kialessa could see, weakly glowing from between the broken antler, the faintest crescent of an aged moon. The dragon was tethered to the wall by a terrifying chain. It was shiny, like steel, and radiated a depressing evil all throughout the dungeon. All along its length sharp spines ran, so that every time the dragon moved the spines cut painfully into its wrist.

The dragon lay breathing in shallow, regretful breaths. Kialessa had no idea how long they stood there, too frightened to move, but eventually it must have caught their scent and it looked up. It regarded them with tired, sad eyes.

'Who are you?' it asked in a weary voice that hid incredible power.

'I am Piex, mighty one,' he said, trembling. 'And this is my servant, Kialessa.'

It lay its great head down on its manacled paw, ignoring them.

'And who,' Piex said, his voice catching in his throat, 'who are you?'

'I forget,' it replied bitterly, its ancient voice lost in a sad sigh.

The dragon was caked in mud, wincing as it adjusted

its position and the terrible chain cut into its wrist once more. But Kialessa had seen that silver sheen in another dragon's scale, and could see the unmistakeable powerful, bearded jaw.

'You … you must be Eclipse's mother. I can't believe the riddle would lead us to you.'

'Eclipse? I do not know that name,' the dragon said with terrible sadness. 'My first clutch was taken away from me eleven years ago, and I have not bred since. Did one of them survive? Perhaps that is well.'

'What are you doing here?' Kialessa asked.

'Why should I tell?' the dragon asked, half sincere.

Carefully, quietly, Kialessa approached the dragon.

'Don't Kia, she's starving,' Piex said.

But somehow Kialessa could not believe that this mighty moon dragon would hurt her, even though she had been chained in a dungeon for at least eleven years.

'It's all right,' she said.

She walked up to the chain. The dragon eyed her suspiciously, but did not eat her once she got close enough, even though she could have swallowed her in one bite. The chain around her arm was huge, and radiated its unyielding evil throughout the cavern. It was terrifying to look at, and Kialessa did not believe she could be made to touch that chain for all the gold in the world. The steel shackles bit into the dragon's swollen arm, cutting it cruelly in several places, deep silver blood still fresh on the wounds. How long had she been made to suffer like this?

It made Kialessa's heart feel sick, to see a mighty creature chained in a dungeon too small to stretch out in. With a tender tear, she placed her hand on the moon dragon's swollen claw.

The dragon breathed in deeply.

'Ahh,' it said with sudden strength. 'You have the touch of **goodness** in you! I have not felt that touch in a long, long time. **Clearly**, you do not have Tobiuus's permission to be down here?'

'We don't.'

'How did you children get mixed up with that archmage?' she asked, her voice now clear and kind.

'He kidnapped us,' Piex said. 'He is my grandfather's brother.'

Kialessa continued to stroke the dragon's injured arm, powerless to do it any more good.

'Ahh,' the dragon sighed. 'So he keeps you a prisoner too? No doubt another attempt at feigning goodness in his dark, sinister heart.'

'He is evil,' Kialessa said.

Piex was silent.

'He is,' the dragon agreed, 'but he can no longer recognise it.'

'Tell me, mighty dragon,' Piex said suddenly, 'is there power in evil?'

The dragon laughed, a gentle sound like a tinkling moonlit waterfall.

'He's been teaching you, hasn't he? And I wonder who taught him? These lies are old, youngling, very, very old. There is power in evil, but it will always lead to suffering and regret in the end. Goodness, properly practiced, will always lead to strength and joy at the last. It really is as simple as that.'

'But Tobiuus teaches us that you need to master them both.'

'He thinks he masters both, doesn't he? But he is blind to his own lies. If he uses evil, his works will lead to suffering and regret. Why embrace such a result, I wonder? Evil is full of temptation, and it has many servants who disguise the results of evil as progress. Tobiuus too, is deceived. To embrace the powers of evil is to eventually bring forth suffering, regression and regret.'

'But can't evil energy be used to work great power?'

'Yes, and it will always lead to remorse and torment,' the dragon replied. 'Evil energy is wickedness: sin, regret, lust, hatred. These things bring about decay and suffering, but they are not such.'

'I see. Yes, I did not know.'

'Do not turn to evil. All that is evil will eventually abandon you, and evil can only be commanded thorough the acts of evil: fear, intimidation, enacting the destruction of another creature's self-worth. Each life, yours and mine, brings forth acts of good and evil until the day we are perfected. Then, when we are full of goodness, we shall see when it is necessary and desirable to cause or allow suffering, to stay our hands from preventing disaster or decay, or to see that the best result for all involved will be to allow the death of one much loved.'

Piex was silent once more.

'Do not harness evil,' said the dragon.

They stood silent in its wisdom.

'My name is Norius,' the dragon said, raising its head to look at them both, 'Please, tell me of this Eclipse. Does one of my children live?'

'Live, and thrive!' Kialessa said. 'We rode –'

'Rode?' Norius questioned. 'She could not be much more than a youngling?'

'Oh no, she's taller than a human adult,' Kialessa said, but the dragon looked sad once more.

'Then her heart is young to be caught inside a body so prematurely developed! Does this Tobiuus know no limits?'

'Seems very few,' Kialessa muttered.

'And she is being taught by the archmage, and raised by her murderous father, Txlax?' the mighty moon dragon asked.

They nodded. The room fell silent, though the mood in the room had lifted, as though the scent of a star crisp evening was stronger now.

Kialessa looked at the kind, wise dragon. Norius was tired and ill. Surely she would die if the chain was not removed soon? Perhaps there was some way.

The dragon seemed to sense Kialessa's thoughts and

smiled at her. 'Do not think to touch the chain, little one. Even a splinter of its evil is too much for one as young as you to bear.'

'Can't you get the chain off?' Kialessa asked, knowing it was hopeless.

'No, it is wholly evil. The only way I can remove it is by becoming evil myself, and I will *not* be tempted to do that. My only hope is that one day the key may be found, or Tobiuus is convinced to free me. But you must not speak to him of our conversation, I am sure he will use it for evil.'

'But there must be something we can do!'

'Not to free me, at least not yet. But there is perhaps another thing I can ask of you. Please children, if you ever have the chance to return, bring my daughter with you. Bring Eclipse. It is not fair to be raised by such evil; she will not have a choice about what she becomes! You must expose her to the truth. Then we will see if her heart has the strength to embrace goodness, or if she must suffer her evil choices a little while longer.'

***

They stayed an hour by the dragon, doing little but comforting her. Then, when their hearts grew too sorry, she made them leave. They were reluctant to do so. Still there was no goblin guarding the desk, and their path back to their room was graciously clear.

'It is a terrible thing to keep that kind moon dragon like that,' Kialessa said out loud once they returned.

Piex pushed his fingers to his lips.

They couldn't even talk about it.

The Imp

'I don't think that chain holds you,' she said. 'Your opinion that you're only capable of evil does.'
– Kialessa, to the imp in the tower.

A key. A key for a dragon.

If there was a key to be found anywhere in the tower, it would surely be in Tobiuus's study, and Kialessa was an expert in sneaking into wizard's studies. At least, she'd **almost** successfully done it once.

But this was too important not to risk it, at least once.

They both knew the best time. The goblins would guard the bedrooms all night, and Piex was expected to be in class with her during the day. So they waited until Tobiuus was out riding his dragon during breakfast, and Kialessa slipped out without anyone seeming to notice.

It was no challenge avoiding the goblins; they were either too busy or too lazy to care. She made her way up to the study door. It was strange; the door was open. She took a quick look around to make sure no one was watching, and slipped in. For a moment, she stood there taking it all in. There were dozens of shelves with hundreds of draws and any one of them could hold a key.

But this key had to be evil.

Immediately she thought of the desk, the one the imp was at. But there was no imp there right now. Perhaps it had escaped? She crept carefully around the room so that she did not alert any unseen guards, and begun to study the desk. She tried not to be nervous, yet she only had a brief time before Tobiuus would return or the students finished breakfast. Either that or a dragon might just happen to fly past the window and see her.

She hurried up to the desk and begun to push open the draws and rifle through them. There were quills, styli, and a thousand other strange devices all in neat arrangements. But no key, and nothing at all that looked or felt particularly evil.

Nothing, except the feather that was sitting on the desk.

A feather. *Well,* she reasoned, *there is no rule saying the key had to be made of metal. She reached out to touch it.*

Without warning the feather unfolded itself out into the shape of the imp, and it grinned its wicked grin.

Kialessa gasped. She'd been found out.

It smiled cruelly, scanning her with its black eyes.

'Good day,' she said, her voice catching her throat.

The imp looked surprised. 'Good day, it says?' the imp thought out loud. 'Trying to make friends?'

'Greetings, imp,' Kialessa said with a little more confidence, since it didn't seem to be planning to attack her.

'What mischief brings you up to the master's desk, I wonders?' it asked her.

'My business.'

The imp looked dissatisfied, but then held out its chain in hope. The chain filled with goodness that kept it locked to this desk; the opposite to the chain that kept a good dragon in a dungeon far below. But Kialessa did not touch the imp's chain either.

'Be lettings me out?' it said. 'I be very helpful!'

'Oh, I know better than that.' She smiled.

'*Please?*'

'No, but do you know where a key is that can unlock a prisoner in the dungeons?'

The imp pouted and sat down. 'I knows not, but what keys the master keeps on himself all the time.'

'Ahh,' Kialessa said. Perhaps he was carrying the key?

'Thank you,' she said, and turned to leave.

'No, no,' the imp begged, then it cawed in cheekiness. 'I know what you dids.' Kialessa stopped. 'You sneaks in here, taking things.'

Kialessa was alarmed and without thinking, covered

its face with her hand.

'But I nots tell, nooo. I nots tell him. Please, please. Release poor Impy and I serve you. Yes, you, for a longs time.'

'No. I can't do that!' she said, and let go, still frightened that the imp would tell.

The imp hurmped, and sat down again.

Then an evil look came over its face. 'Then I screams now. He be very angry. I cry out and he come running, he and all the students. Then what wills you do, mmm? Then where you hide in here?'

7 Imps are trouble!

Kialessa's palms started sweating; this little creature was driving a hard bargain. But she could also tell that it was frightened. Despite all its threats, it was frightened too.

'No,' she repeated sternly, being bold. 'I will *not* free you.'

'Nooo,' it wailed. 'You are cruel. Too cruel! You not imprison Impy, we lives forever. Ever! Too long to be alone. See, Impy knows things you not ever know. Seen whole history of world from start, I haves. Knows things, hidden things. The birthing of the gods, the filling the sky with air and land with life! I sees the wars that made evil, and the rise and fall of the golden city. I know, I have *seen*.'

Such knowledge was tempting, but Kialessa knew that even the truth could be a lie in the mouth of a demon.

'No. No deal. You stay, I'm leaving.'

'Nooo!' it begged. 'He be harsh! He uses me to tell him evil secrets, ones that burn. I hates the secrets, they are pain. Please, please let me go.'

That gave her an idea, and since it seemed to be a good idea to keep the imp talking, at least for now, she dared to ask, 'What do you say evil is then, little imp?'

The imp looked smug then, content to show off. Its eyes flickered about, as if it was reading a book, or perhaps a tome of some forgotten lore. 'Here be the words of Chammah, a blithling wizard,' and here its voice took on a much more formal tone. 'Perversion is the true nature of evil. True evil takes something unworthy, and makes it appear good to the soul. Then it takes that which is designed to bring life and health, and calls it unpopular, even unwholesome. The purest evil will then never willingly admit it has ever done wrong. It will cause tyranny, whisper regret, make a bad decision seem necessary or even praiseworthy. It will then take its victims and hound them unceasingly with their own mistakes. But never, never, will it claim any blame for itself. "I am right, I am pure, I have done no wrong," it will say, a diabolical perversion of all that is true.'

Then the imp fell silent.

Fascinating, thought Kialessa.

She wanted to share the imp's words with Piex, but she was wary. After all, it was an imp. But then she realised, it could also deceive her by telling her the truth, knowing she did not trust it. She would then be tricked into rejecting something that was good.

The thought twisted her mind in knots. In the end, she reasoned, it was probably just trying to win her trust so that she would set it free.

But how free was the imp, when it was still a prisoner to its own nature? Then Kialessa had an idea, and idea inspired by the imp's own words.

'I will not release you, but why do you not release yourself?'

The creature looked up in surprise and hope.

'All your life, your entire existence you've used evil. What if you were to try goodness? Then surely the holy chain would slip off your heel like butter on a hot knife.'

It was what the dragon had said would work for her. If her evil chain could be removed by becoming evil, then surely this imp could remove its chain by becoming good. The creature looked hopeful, then sunk down low again.

'It not work. I wholly evil, nothing more. Sad, hurting evil. I be burnt up by goodness if I even think about it!'

'Well, how do you know?'

'HE told me. The demon god. His name I never speak.'

'This demon god, does he ever lie?'

'He never not lies.'

'Then maybe it's a lie that becoming good will kill you.'

The imp had to think about that.

'Try it,' she said. 'Do something kind, or help someone. I dunno, save someone's life! I am good, but see, my touch does not burn you.'

Then she patted it. At first, it was terrified, then it warmed at her touch.

'I don't think that chain holds you,' she said. 'Your opinion that you're only capable of evil does.'

The imp said nothing. For what must have been the first time in its existence, it was silent.

Kialessa smiled, and then left as quickly as she could.

***

Days passed, yet there was no way Kialessa could think of to search Tobiuus's robes. *Maybe if he is asleep? Or maybe if a lucky chance presents itself?* But still nothing happened. For now, freeing Norius the moon dragon appeared to mean waiting for a miracle.

Eventually Dusk called on Piex to do another menial chore – he was fond of doing that. But Piex had learnt not to complain, and the other students had learnt it made no difference to how quickly Piex mastered magic. So Piex picked up a satchel of herbs and flower petals, handed them to Kialessa, and led the way up the stairs to Tobiuus's study.

Maybe this would be their chance.

She and Piex walked up the precisely cut stone steps to the thick oak door clasped in iron bands and covered in silent sigils of arcane power. Kialessa heard voices behind that door, and she instantly recognised one of them. With a silent gasp she held Piex back from opening the door.

It was Dog.

The intruder, the cruel man. The man who she had stopped when he'd tried to assassinate her king. It was *him*, here – and he was talking to Tobiuus!

All her priorities changed. Carefully, she slipped in without making a sound. Then she indicated to Piex that he should remain here as a distraction if she needed it.

Almost not daring to breathe, she crept towards them. She only just caught the end of their conversation.

'… and you needn't crush my thongsweed when you sit down, Jerik,' the archmage ordered.

'Oh! Sorry, your eminence,' he said, his voice snide, as

if it held a secret over all those who heard it. 'There's just so much mess around here right now. It makes it hard for poor, uneducated folk like meself to know where it's safe to sit.'

'You are far from uneducated, my cunning interlocutor. And as for being poor, well you mustn't be counting the excessive sum I paid you for your supplies this morning.'

'Well,' he said with what sounded like a smile, 'such supplies are so hard to come by, aren't they, especially the poisons.'

The archmage huffed. 'I assure you; such is not my intent. They are merely rare and valuable spell components for my research …'

'Oh, of that I had no doubt. But tell me, what is it that you've brought me up here to see?'

The archmage pointed to a scroll on the table at the foot of the imp.

The cruel man reached out, then pulled back as if the paper itself was dangerous to him.

Tobiuus grinned. 'As you requested; the instructions for contacting a wisp demon. I do not care to know what you wish to use it for, but I should warn that wisp demons are particularly subtle and only a fool would consider it. Also, as requested; the ritual is not complete. You will need to make sure you protect yourself properly.'

The assassin caressed the paper, careful not to open it. 'Oh, it's not for me. I know someone that will pay handsomely for this information.'

'Hmmm,' the archmage replied, then turned away with distain.

'Well!' Dog said in a cheery voice, standing up, 'if our business here is all complete?'

'Prudent silence would be wise,' the archmage warned.

Dog stood up and skipped to the doorway. 'Naturally. You know me. Living out here, past the western forests, a man needs to know how to keep his silence. But now all this quiet is boring me, and if you don't mind, I've some debts I'd like to pay off with this little fortune you've given me.'

'You will forget this conversation,' the archmage said, and Kialessa felt the imposition of magic in his words.

Dog opened his mouth, but the archmage hushed him. 'If you cannot keep silence, assassin, I shall be forced to turn you into a snake, then everyone can see what a forked tongue you really have.'

Dog smiled. 'Very well, you are correct, as always. Still, I must be going now.'

He skipped past Kialessa without seeming to notice her and on to the door.

Rage boiled up inside her. He had not answered for his crimes against King Dunnkan, and now here he was, selling poisons to Tobiuus! Someone had to stop him.

She waited till he swung open the door, with an 'oh' as he almost ran smack into Piex. He paused there, just for an instant, just long enough for Kialessa to run her whip from its hook and lash out at him.

Without even turning around he caught it mid-air.

Then he turned, looking at her with first surprise, then amusement. 'Hello, young one.' He said, like this was an old conversation among friends.

'Oh,' said Tobiuus, looking at the scene with interest, 'I see you've met my nephew's impetuous servant.'

'We've met,' the man said with a cruel, twisted smile. He did not let go of her whip as he fingered his deep scar on his right cheek, and now Kialessa could see it was a disfigured symbol of the royal crest.

'Why?' she demanded to know. 'What I want to know is *why* do you tried to kill our king?'

Piex was right behind him and could have stabbed him in the back, or done *something*. But he didn't move.

The man she called Dog said nothing.

'Evil,' she accused him, still holding to her whip as firmly as she could.

He looked sad, then smiled again as he let the whip slip from his fingers. 'Oh, you know what that is, then? Do you have the right to say what is right or wrong, young one? You look at me as if in killing me you'd rid the world of a great evil, but can you truly be so sure? I have spared your life on many occasions …'

She thought before answering. 'You're confusing the issue, and not answering my question.'

'Who can really say what is right or wrong in this

world? It will surprise you, one day, to learn what is really going on here – perhaps even break your heart. What if, in preventing me from ending the king's life then, you only ensured a greater disaster would follow? Maybe *you* are the evil one here.'

She gasped at his suggestion, and if she'd had the means, would have cut the cruel smirk from his face that instant.

But he just smiled at her indignation, and with a courteous bow, and no answers, skipped out.

Tobiuus ignored the whole incident, and Kialessa didn't hear much of what he and Piex talked about, she was so upset. But she went to bed with bitter thoughts that evening of the evil that seemed to flock to this place so easily, and that would, if it could, keep her here forever. Yet, because of the magic, by the next morning she'd forgotten the entire conversation, but not her feelings, which gnawed at her almost constantly now:

Had they truly been forgotten?

The dream

*I do not know all the reasons for suffering in this world, but I do know this: that the question you must ask of deity is not **why**, but **what** you will do with the situation you are given. Will you honour your gods with your choices, even in the midst of sorrow and pain you are called upon to endure?*

– Plarros, 6th Sage of Lumos, keeper of times.

That night, Kialessa had a strange dream.

She was walking into the college, briefly wondering how she'd gotten there. For a tiny moment she was ecstatic to think they'd escaped somehow, but that thought felt strange. Yet the college, the students, the sights and sounds were all exactly as she remembered it that winter. How she missed it now that she wasn't allowed to attend!

There, standing at the door of her class, was the headmistress, keeper of the children.

'Kia,' she said, 'where have you been?'

'Oh,' Kialessa replied, getting upset, 'Uncle Tobiuus has been keeping me. I've been trying to come to class, but he's got us locked up in a tower so very far away and we don't know how to get out!'

The headmistress looked puzzled, and seemed to be about to send her into class, when Kialessa heard someone call her name.

It was Kiel, her brother, or her sort of brother, since he really was a slave her mother bought off a stranger several years back. He was about her same age.

'Kiel!' she said with an excited smile.

'I thought you'd never get here. They've been looking all over for you.'

Just then the dream became very vivid, and she realised for the first time that she was dreaming.

'We are dreamwalking again,' she said.

'Of course, come on. You'll get lost here without me. There are things I want you to see.'

They walked off, leaving the headmistress standing there, handing out red tea-cup flowers to the other students. Suddenly, they were standing in the field where she often practiced swordplay. There were only two people there now, a young man swinging a sword in powerful, skilled strokes, and an auburn enchantress that

Kialessa knew very well.

'Darrix, Allastassia!' she cried, and ran up to them. But they didn't act as if they heard her, and when she went to hug them, she walked right through them.

'This happened this morning,' Kiel said.

'Darrix,' Allastassia complained, 'come to dinner, you need food.'

Darrix smiled, and kept hitting the pole with his wooden sword. 'Not tonight.'

'You fast too much. You can't let waiting for them kill you as well!'

He lowered his sword. 'They're all right, I know it,' he said. 'And when the time comes to free them, I'm going to help. I'm going to be the best I can be so that when King Dunnkan asks for volunteers to take on the dragon and the wizard, I'll be ready.'

Allastassia looked flustered. 'You can't take on a dragon, Darrix.'

'Not yet.' He kept hitting the pole with his sword.

'It could be years,' she said. 'Anyway, I hear there is a new expedition taking off in a few days, I suppose you'll be going with them. So I'll go with them as well.'

'That is good of you.'

'It's been a long wait. We can't keep missing college.' She walked off.

'He will keep that up till we're found, won't he?' Kialessa said to Kiel.

'Yes, I think he will. He is one of your friends. And so

is that enchantress. She too, is preparing. But I think you have another friend you need to see.'

They were in the forest now, and it was dark. Kialessa had no idea how Kiel was able to do all this, walk them around in a dream like it was his own personal window on reality.

A lonely character was drinking at a stream, bending down to drink directly from it. It was Posk. Then he picked up a stick and drew something in the mud by the river. She went to look at it, knowing she could not reach him, and Posk acted as though they weren't even there.

It was two stick figures, one was shorter than the other, and the taller one had two little points on its head: like horns.

'He misses me to?' Kialessa smiled sadly.

'He doesn't trust himself without you,' Kiel said. 'He hasn't been at the college at all since you were taken.'

'Oh Posk,' she said sadly, wishing he could hear her. 'We're all right. We'll be back soon. You shouldn't skip on education just because your friends aren't there.'

As they watched, Posk drew a single line from her hand to his neck. Then he muttered two words again and again: 'Lessa. *Tauira-Toa.*'

Then with a sudden, guttural roar, Posk threw his head back and howled into the night. He punched his fist into his mud drawing and ran off into the darkness.

The sight made Kialessa sad. 'Oh, Kiel, why are you showing me all this?'

He smiled. 'To bring you comfort. I've been watching them trying to find you. So many seek to free you! Let me show you.'

The next thing she knew they were standing in King Dunnkan's throne room. The entire elite guard were there; as well as the steward, the wizard, the captain and the priestess. King Dunnkan was there too, the crown on his head, the sceptre in his hands.

'I think this happens tonight,' Kiel said. Could he really dream into the future?

'We've searched the entire eastern frontier,' the steward said, 'and all the reports from the scouts and rangers in the area report nothing about a wizard riding a rot dragon. We cannot continue without encroaching on troll lands.'

'Will they let us in?' the wizard asked.

'Not without payment, and not with a guarantee that our men will be safe.'

'So,' the captain said, 'we cannot search out troll lands until we know for sure they are there, and even then, only in great numbers.'

'Still, we have not yet ruled out that the wizard took them to the plaintiff islands. While pirates are common in the area–' the steward started.

'Have you forgotten,' the captain stated tersely, 'that two griffon riding trolls assisted the wizard? I still maintain that our best option is to search further into troll territory.'

'An option which, after all this time, has yet to produce fruit, need I remind *you*?' The steward clenched his fist.

The king held his hands up for peace. 'Gentles, please, we are all in need of patience.'

'My liege, you are correct,' the steward said with a tactful bow, 'but it has been almost a half-season, we cannot continue to commit so many resources to these two children or else the late spring harvests will go undermanned.'

'In this, I do agree,' the Priestess replied. 'If patience is what is called for, then perhaps we'd do best awaiting the will of the Eternal before attempting to proceed further. I am of good conscience that I have yet done all I can do.'

'As am I,' the wizard agreed with a nod of his head, as did several others in the room.

There was silence, and the king sighed as though the weight of a world rested on his shoulders. Then he spoke, 'And is there any news from the Wytch of the Wayst?'

'No, sire,' the priestess replied.

The king looked surprised, then despondent. 'We do not abandon the search,' he declared in an official tone, 'but make sure all the harvests are gathered in, keep the kingdom running, do what you must. But we do not abandon the search. Plus, double the bounty.'

The steward and others seemed surprised, but did not argue with the will of their king.

'You may have done all you can, but I have not,' King Dunnkan said. 'Return to your duties.' He seemed tired, and looked as though he had not been sleeping well.

Kialessa felt a pang of fear. Had they just given up looking for them?

Slowly, everyone left. Everyone except the priestess.

The king motioned for her to follow him. Kialessa and Kiel went with them. The next moment, they were inside the small chapel to the Eternal that King Dunnkan kept near his throne room and in which he and his family alone, with perhaps a few nobles, were permitted to worship each Serrosday. At least it showed that they were careful about the king's security in that way.

The king went and knelt before the golden circle of the Eternal.

'Priestess,' the king began, his head bowed, 'I have not failed to pray both night and day for the children. In all my life, I've never been so concerned for ones so young. And yet, for all the danger I fear, I only feel peace. Why is this?'

'As my prayers have also told me,' the priestess said, standing beside the king, gazing up at the circle as well, 'the children are safe, and the time of their deliverance is not yet, but soon. I am confident they will be all right, and well cared for within the all-seeing view of the Eternal's love.'

'That is good,' the king replied. 'But my people grow weary of this search, and I know it is unwise to push them much further. How long must we wait? Will they be delivered soon? And by whom, and how?'

        By Dr Joseph Ireland "Dr Joe"

The priestess smiled. 'These things are not for us to say. When we have done all that we can do, then we must stand by, and have faith that a perfect God knows how to reply in His own good way, and in His own good time.'

The king pondered this. 'I do not know why this had to happen, but I do know what I have to do: wait.'

'And that is more than enough.'

'Deliverance *will come*,' King Dunnkan promised himself.

'I agree,' the priestess said to the king, and left him to his prayers.

'I agree too,' Kiel said to Kialessa as the dream began to fade into a misty wilderness.

Kialessa began to panic as she saw the dream coming to an end. 'But what of my father, does he know? And how long till we're set free? How long?'

Kiel smiled kindly as he let the world go, and it was his kindness that left a warm glow in her heart as she woke up on her bed of straw again.

In the floating distance between dreams and waking up she heard her king's voice. 'Not long now, but if it were forever that you had to wait, young Kialessa, the question is not *why*, but *what* you will do with the opportunities you are given, and the time that is allotted to you. Be patient, be brave, be good. Sometimes the best thing we can do is simply wait, and rely upon the simple faith that it will all work out in the end.'

The angel

Never lose hope! Never lose sight of your goal, and eventually you will find a way. Without hope, you will surrender to an inferior foe. Without hope, you will quit in the middle of a test you would have passed. Only those prisoners without hope will be blind to the opportunity of escape …

– High Priestess of the Eternal, castle records, 15.2.312 CY

'What are you studying?' Kialessa asked Piex that evening.

Piex sighed and put his stylus down.

'It's summoning, part of the Curatium Hall of magic. Very difficult stuff.' He wiped his brow.

She looked at his spell book, but it was all

Dragonspeech to her. Strange symbols that hinted at great magic were scrawled all over the pages. Somehow, within those symbols and their meanings, was the magic that Piex was mastering.

'Teach me those, too,' she asked.

'You are always going to be curious, aren't you?'

'You bet.' She loved picking up a little magic here and there. Besides, she knew something that Piex hadn't realised; he liked to teach. She could tell when he needed a break from his study.

'You know, I've been thinking about what happened in the kitchen,' he said.

'What do you suppose went wrong?'

'You somehow managed to create an open spell, *like* sorcery. It was very dangerous. I don't know how you did it, but you were drawing all the magic out of the automaton, and me. I must look into it one day. You definitely need more training.'

'So train me. Tell me how it all works.'

He smiled, and sat forwards to begin his lecture. 'The whole universe is composed of five great qualities.' His fingers dancing out patterns in the air to illustrate his words. 'Everything in the universe is made up of qualities which can be roughly translated as: flow, time, matter, life and consciousness. The last four all have various amounts of flow, gathering and dispersing, making up the eight halls of magic we discussed last time. This is how we create manifestations of magic.'

'Is gathering the same as goodness, and dispersing the same as evil?'

'No, and I think that's where most of the confusion comes from. Gathering produces light, and light can sometimes mean truth, and that often also means goodness. But light can also mean shining, and that just means well-lit. Sometimes, in that sense, darkness is more useful, especially if you're trying to fall to sleep, or hide from enemies, etcetera.'

Kialessa paused. 'Maybe that's where your uncle is getting it wrong. There is an opposite for everything, just like he said. But deliberately being evil to "balance" your goodness? That just sounds wrong.'

Piex pondered that, but didn't have an answer.

'Still,' Kialessa said, 'all this magic is amazing. How did they come up with it?'

'They didn't. It is believed the gods released magic into the world thousands of years ago to enhance their power of creation. Years later, one of the first races, the Ancients, created the language of dragons to harness magic for themselves and others. Most of what we wizards do is try to learn what they already knew, get back some of the glory of the Golden Age. Most of the magic that the Ancients held is long lost, only a few scattered pages and hidden clues are left. Wizards have had to piece everything else together since then. But here is a little something found by the first wizards hundreds of years ago, rumoured to be recovered from the ruins of

Civit Aurea by the hand of an unknown mage.'

He turned a page and there was a picture, an ornate circle with many strange symbols along the outside.

'What is it?' she asked.

'The summoning grid,' he replied. 'It is very important to get it right every time, or you may die.'

Her hand leapt off the page, just in case.

'Whenever you perform a summoning,' he explained, smiling, 'you need the creature to appear inside one of these or it will not be bound to your will. That's very important, especially when summoning elementals or … demons.'

Neither of them wanted that, but both knew Tobiuus had performed the spell for that purpose many times.

'What's the other circle for?' Kialessa asked.

'For yourself, for protection. Sometimes that's not even enough because you could get drawn back into the place you're summoning creatures from, or they can break your control and attack you.'

Kialessa was glad that she wasn't a wizard. 'Do you need to know all this off by heart?'

'That's why we use spell books!'

Kialessa was troubled. 'You don't think your uncle will make you summon a demon, do you?' She knew how dangerous, illegal and self-destructive it would be to summon a demon.

'I do not doubt it,' Piex said, not looking up. Clearly he'd given it some previous thought, and it was not a thought he enjoyed. 'You know how he's all about this "balance between good and evil" thing.'

She did, but then she hit on a clever plan. 'You don't suppose he'd make you summon an angel too, then?'

Piex looked up at her, realising what she was implying.

But they said nothing out loud about planning to summon in an angel to rescue them.

There were too many spies.

***

One week went by, and Piex was called, as he occasionally was, to the study. Kialessa figured that Uncle Tobiuus had something he wanted to show off again. It was disappointing to them both to find Dusk there too, his dark automaton waiting, unmoving, behind him.

'Good, you are all here,' Tobiuus said. 'Apprentices, stand back, we will now practice the summoning sub-college of Curatium magic. Piex, as lesser apprentice, you may go first.'

Kialessa could tell it was the moment he had dreaded. He cast his magical armour first on himself, then on Kialessa.

Dusk smothered a giggle at these preparations, and Tobiuus glared at the older apprentice.

Piex stood up boldly to his uncle's detailed summoning grid, where the formidable protections helped to shield Tobiuus's castle from most of the damage the students could do. Then, with a confident, *'Aer elementum, i eligere te!'* Piex cast his summoning spell.

A wind twisted in the centre of the circle, then suddenly burst into wild tornado, no higher than Kialessa's knee. It moved about as though it was alive. It reminded her of the fire that she'd defeated last spring, when saving her king. Then, after twenty or so instants, the air died and the whirlwind disappeared.

'Adequate,' Tobiuus said. 'First apprentice, your turn.'

Dusk was grinning, as though he'd already won even before he'd started moving into the summoning grid. The air shimmered in the circle and a wave of burning heat filled the room for a moment. There was a brief crack like the splitting of stone and a red fissure formed in mid-air, spouting fire. In the middle of the fire, stood a dog.

It was no ordinary dog. It was almost the size of a posk, with burning eyes and fire for breath. It roared at Dusk in a strange language, and he laughed at it. The hound paced back and forth, roaring menacingly at everyone in the room. It threatened Piex and Kialessa, who watched it in wonder as it strained against the invisible barrier that held it.

'With this magic, he could command this torment wolf to tear you limb from limb, and it gladly would,' Tobiuus mocked. 'Is not this *power*?'

Piex said nothing.

Then the bright shield shimmered and a waft of the

wolf's fiery breath escaped. Tobiuus watched his first apprentice with a menacing glare in his eyes, for failure was not tolerated at his college. He seemed to be preparing to draw something from his robes.

But the older apprentice struggled against the beast's will and brought it back under control. Then he dismissed it with a wave of his hands. With a roar of displeasure, it disappeared back into hell.

Tobiuus's voice was cold and threatening. 'The spell was of your own choosing, but your control was lacking. Do not exceed yourself for pride, boy. It will kill you.' He seemed only just able to hold himself back from a more severe rebuke.

Dusk held his head up with pride, but not arrogance. Kialessa could tell he knew just how great the wizardry was that he had worked.

But Tobiuus had not finished with his chastisement. He pulled a scroll from the shelves and handed it to Piex.

'Real mastery, true mastery, is a matter of time and patience. However, another factor is often involved, that of talent. Piex, cast this spell.'

Piex scanned the scroll with almost superhuman speed. It was huge.

'What is it?' Kialessa whispered.

'Another summoning, of the fifth order,' Piex said. 'Mine was of the first order, Dusk's of the third. This scroll alone is worth over two thousand gold coins, and it is only good for a single casting!'

'And he uses it to correct his student?' Kialessa marvelled at the way his uncle tossed around a lifetime's worth of wealth at a whim.

'What I wouldn't give to keep this –'

'Silence!' Tobiuus roared. 'Cast! And concentrate, youngling, or it may be your last.'

It was their chance, and Piex knew it. If Tobiuus had planned for Piex to summon another demon he was about to be disappointed. As Piex chanted, a soft glow filled the room, dispelling the lingering essences of greed and violence that had accompanied the torment wolf. With a sudden burst of a radiant trumpet, an angel appeared, forged from the solar essence of the sun god from time immemorial. A huge pair of golden feathered wings unfolded to reveal a powerful human-like form. Across her back a large golden scythe was slung, no doubt waiting to be unsheathed at any moment and plunged through the beating hearts of the wicked. Around her a daunting nimbus of dark blue light shone, filling every good heart with confidence, and every evil heart with terror.

'Who has summoned me from the ambrosial fields to face the forces of evil?' she asked in a quiet voice that inspired both courage and fear.

'Fool,' Dusk said. 'There is no challenge in this! An angel will not test its bounds.'

'I would not presume such a thing, especially in a place such as this,' Tobiuus said.

'I thought the fulcrum, the angel to balance the wolf …' Piex muttered, straining with all his will to confine the powerful magic that was well beyond his years to master. The scroll had been written by his uncle, so a portion of his uncle's power was in the spell to help him, but it was still an enormous challenge.

'Indeed,' Tobiuus said. 'Perhaps you *are* learning.'

Kialessa, however, saw an opportunity. Perhaps it was the opportunity that Piex had intended to give her. For a brief moment she thought about 'accidentally' breaking Piex's concentration and releasing the angel, but Tobiuus would surely be too powerful for that, and too well prepared. But if angels were kind …

Help us! She mouthed to the angel as she laid eyes on her. *We're prisoners!*

The angel looked at her for a moment, and without giving away her secret, continued to look around the room.

'Why have you brought me here?' She suddenly roared. 'Surely young wizards have better things to do with their time than to match their skill against divine foes!'

'I assure you, angel, we have no need of such entertainment,' Tobiuus said. 'Don't waste my scroll, Piex. You summoned it, ask it some questions.'

'Who are you?' the angel demanded of Piex.

'He's Piex, and he will become the greatest wizard in all the Great Kingdom,' Kialessa shouted.

'It is we who ask the questions here, servant! Bite your tongue, least I have it bitten for you,' Tobiuus snapped.

'Forgive me, Lord Tobiuus,' she said as quickly as she could.

Tobiuus, ignoring her any further, smiled to himself.

Kialessa knew he felt every wizard should have their admirers and servants, and that it was her job to fill this role for his favourite pupil. What the great archmage did not realise, however, was she'd just told the angel his name.

Hastily, Piex posed a few questions to the summoned angel while she prowled against the magical field. They were honest research questions about the dimension the angel had come from and the sorts of things apprentice wizards should know.

Suddenly the field began to waver.

'Concentrate, boy.' Tobiuus said.

Steeling his mind, Piex asked the question that plagued him the most. 'What do you say evil is?'

The angel smiled, glancing over at Tobiuus. 'There are many kinds of evil in this world, young wizard, and it wise to know and reject them all. However, very few people pursue evil for its own sake. Most are deceived into thinking their way is good, such as the ancient troll warlord Toto-Muru. They are all deceived, for to do evil while naming it good is a fruitless and *vain* act.'

The angel continued, 'There are those, however, who openly admit to being evil. They revel in it, unrepentant.

Perhaps they think they have no soul to lose. Perhaps they think there is no eternal repercussion for their sins. Or perhaps they fear they have already earned the worst that hell has to offer, and another sin cannot add to their eternal suffering. Do not listen to their words, boy, for they are as poison. Listen instead to the voice that guides toward truth, and – '

Suddenly, mid-sentence, the angel threw herself against the field. With a terrifying explosion she breached the weakest part of it, and without pausing to hold her wounds, she leapt towards Piex, a desperate look in her eyes.

'Tobiuus!' Piex screamed in fright.

His uncle watched the angel fly towards Piex, waiting till she was only a hand away from touching him. Then with a swift dismissive gesture, he unleashed a wave of magical energy. Before their very eyes, she dissipated like glistening dust.

But not before she had whispered something to Piex. Something that sounded like a language, but it was soft and airy, like the wind.

Tobiuus laughed. 'Three moments! Such talent. Good, good, very good.'

Dusk snapped in anger. 'He had the scroll to help him, did he not? And it was an **angel**.'

Tobiuus's look silenced him.

'Forgive me, master,' Dusk cunningly apologised, a clever smile on his lips. 'But I realise the angel is capable of teleporting those it touches.'

Tobiuus's look darkened.

Perhaps he was wondering if Piex hadn't "accidently" lost control after all.

'Indeed. He did fail,' Tobiuus said, a quiet regret in his voice. Uttering a single word of power a huge blast of dark energy washed across them. She and Piex tried to resist the magic, but Tobiuus was too powerful. It tore all the strength and stamina from their bodies. Piex crashed to the floor, and Kialessa stumbled on her feet. Her vision darkened so much she could only see what she looked at directly.

'Leave us, and learn from this,' Tobiuus said sternly, but then began to laugh again as they stumbled exhausted out the study door.

'I can't keep this up forever,' Piex muttered as they closed the door and leaned on each other, making their way slowly down the stairs.

'You won't have to. What did that angel say?'

'What do you mean?' Piex asked.

'Didn't you hear it? It was something like, *Amynedd, ni re comming.*'

'Really?' he said, disbelieving. 'That's air speech! The speech of air beings. I forgot angels can speak all languages. It means "Patience. We are coming".'

'Who, the angels?'

'I hope so. I really do,' he replied, sounding hopeful for the first time since they'd arrived.

The dragons

The dragon looked down at her with the profound wisdom of age. 'Oh, I do not complain. Though suffering is not always easy to bear, all suffering has purpose. One day you will understand. I am here for reasons that goes far beyond Tobiuus's petty plans, I assure you.'

'What reasons?' Eclipse asked.

'I do not yet know,' the moon dragon said in a voice as calm and still as a moonlit ocean.

– Norius, moon dragon, cited by Piex. Castle records 63.2.313 CY

Three more days passed, and Piex was now second apprentice. Kialessa had told him about her dream, and so they waited. Their goals had changed. They weren't looking directly for a way to escape, they were waiting to be rescued, and in the meantime they were looking for a way to help Norius, the moon dragon, to escape. They hadn't found the key yet, but perhaps they could keep a promise. They had to tell Eclipse about her mother and show her the truth about Tobiuus's evil.

That evening they were up on the roof again, trying to entice the rot dragons to take them for a ride. Piex had finally gotten on one the week before, but did not enjoy it in the least, and as the dragon had put him down it whacked him on the back with its wing. From that time on he begged Kialessa with his eyes to not try so hard to get him a ride.

But Tobiuus could be watching.

Kialessa stood out on the ledge, hair flying in the cold breeze that flowed from the northern mountains at night, and dared to whisper a single name. She hoped no other dragon could hear her. 'Eclipse, we need you. There's something you need to see.'

But Eclipse did not come that evening, and a feisty young rot dragon stole the pickled rat from Kialessa's stick before she could get a ride for her wizard. Piex looked so relieved about that! They went back down pretending to be disappointed like the others who'd missed out on a ride.

They sat in silence in their room. Kialessa had noticed over the past few weeks that Piex was becoming increasingly moody, and dealt with it by absorbing himself in his studies. Kialessa could see he was beginning to lose hope of a rescue. It had been so long. With an agitated grunt he picked up a dark covered book, *Nefarion's Maleficent Incantations*, that he'd been ignoring as much as possible.

'Patience, they're coming,' she said while she polished his boots.

He sighed, and put the book back down, replacing it with his own journal. They were coming, she was sure of it. They *had* to be. They …

Is this our life now? she caught herself wondering.

There was an unexpected knock at the door.

Kialessa jumped up to open it and in rushed a young girl she'd never seen before. She was about Kialessa's age. Her hair was black as night and completely straight, and her pale skin had just a hint of silver.

The girl stood there, smiling, as though waiting for them to recognise her. Her eyes were bright and her irises a shining moon-grey colour.

'Who are you?' Kialessa asked.

'Don't tell me you can't work it out? Oh, I am getting better at this!' she said in a voice that sounded so familiar, but Kialessa could not work out where she'd heard it before.

'Eclipse?' Piex ventured.

'Very good,' she said. 'So maybe I'm not so good.'

'Eclipse?' Kialessa gasped in surprise and disbelief. 'How can it be? What has Tobiuus –'

'Tobiuus,' the young girl said with anger and disgust,

        By Dr Joseph Ireland "Dr Joe"

as she looked around the room, 'has nothing to do with my being here. As far as I'm aware, he does not even know I possess the power of a human form.'

Her voice sounded strange, too confident to be the young human she looked like. Kialessa began to feel a bit nervous.

'Still, it's fascinating,' Eclipse said, walking in front of Piex's mirror to take a look at herself. 'I appear to take on more of my real age once I take human form.'

Kialessa stepped closer to get a better look. She looked just like a human, but inside her eyes there was a vigour and confidence that made her look just a little more … deadly.

'You look just like a human,' Kialessa said, with a little reverence. Dragons were some of the oldest creatures on the world, respected for their power and consulted worldwide for the wisdom. To have one in the room was terrifying.

'I am human, for now,' Eclipse replied. 'It's something I can do. A trait I inherited from my mother, no doubt.'

'Aren't you afraid Tobiuus will find you here?' Kialessa asked.

'Not at all. What, you think he has nothing better to do than to scry on your room all night? You'd be lucky if he does that once a season. No, he gets all his information from the crafty goblins that listen at your doors, and I took care of them. Come and see.'

They followed the dragon out into the hall and there

were the goblin guards, all sleeping soundly.

'I used an enchantment that can cause sleep, much like the breath of a star dragon. My breath, in dragon form, causes frost or paralysation. Sometimes it can be used to calm others, another gift from my mysterious mother.'

8 Kialessa and Eclipse (human form)

'Yes, about your mother,' Piex began.

Kialessa waved him to silence. 'That's amazing, but won't Tobiuus still find out you were here?'

'Yes, and when he does I'll tell him about the pickled rats I stole. It should convince him and he probably won't even punish me. He approves of tests of stealth. If anyone cops a whipping it'll be those greedy goblins!' She laughed out loud.

'Now,' Eclipse said, turning herself around to look at them. 'My father gave me quite the beating once he learnt I let a non-wizard ride with me. But I want to know if it was worth it. What do you want to speak to me about?'

Piex was about to speak again, but Kialessa didn't let him. 'I think there's something very important you need to see.'

Eclipse shrugged.

Kialessa couldn't help but stare, she looked *just* like a human. Even the eyes, well, that wasn't *so* unusual.

'If you insist. Where is it?'

'Down here.' Kialessa began to lead the way down to the dungeon. Eclipse seemed to have unparalleled skill in keeping silent, her bare feet made no sound at all as she followed them through the doors and down the stairs. They even made it past the kitchens without trouble. They came to the storage room, and Kialessa used the magic word to cause the stairs to appear.

But the desk was guarded, and the goblin called out a greeting once the stairs opened to his lair.

'What do we do now?' Piex whispered.

'I could eat him?' Eclipse suggested, a playful smile curling on the edge of her mouth.

'No,' Kialessa said. 'We just need to distract him, just for a moment. We'll get in with no trouble at all then.'

Eclipse huffed in disappointment.

'Perhaps I'll try out a new enchantment I learnt,' Piex said, and when no one disagreed, he began.

It was a simple illusion, a figment that made a profoundly realistic echo of Tobiuus's voice from down the hall. 'Guard, come hither!'

Without hesitation, the goblin dropped its stylus and hastened out.

The three of them rushed into the room and Piex began working on the prison door again.

Eclipse sniffed. 'There is a fenwright in one of these rooms.'

The next moment, Piex had the dragon's door open and they hastened in.

Inside it was dark once more.

'Who is there?' Norius's kind, yet pain-filled voice requested.

'We are,' Kialessa replied, and told Piex to make his light.

As soon as it lit up, Eclipse's fear-filled gasp echoed across the chamber, and she threw herself back against the wall. Piex's white/blue light shimmered across the glistening, mud-soaked scales, and the chained dragon sat up blinking.

'My child!' Norius suddenly whispered in disbelief, as she saw the shaped-changed dragon.

'No,' Eclipse said, her voice struggling to find words.

Norius must have sensed her distress and sat back down. For a long time, there was silence.

'Who, who are you?' Eclipse whispered.

The moon dragon laughed. 'Is that what **all** you kids want to know nowadays?' She adjusted her arm painfully. 'I must assume you are not an illusion come to deceive me; your scent seems real. And you have asked an honest question, so I will give you what I feel to be an honest answer. I am a prisoner of Tobiuus. I have been these past eleven years since the forced hatching of my first clutch to the black monster Txlax. I am Norius, and if you are Eclipse, you are my daughter.'

Eclipse burst into tears. 'No! It's not true. You cannot be! You abandoned me at birth. Tobiuus told me.'

'If I abandoned you, it is because this chain prevents me from taking you to the wind–'

'Mother,' Eclipse wept, and flung herself at the great moon dragon.

The mother dragon winced as the chain gashed into her wrist, but she wrapped her arms around her crying daughter as best as she could. 'My child, my child.'

Piex struggled to keep back the tears, but Kialessa let them fall. Norius looked up at them and smiled. She was holding her daughter for the first time.

Eclipse looked at the chain. 'It's not right for him to make you suffer like this,' she said, her voice fierce and dangerous.

The dragon looked down at her with the profound wisdom of age. 'Oh, I do not complain. Though suffering is not always easy to bear, all suffering has purpose. One day you will understand. I am here for reasons that goes far beyond Tobiuus's petty plans, I assure you.'

'What reasons?' Eclipse asked.

'I do not yet know,' the moon dragon said in a voice as calm and still as a moonlit ocean.

Eclipse gasped in disbelief.

'I'm glad you have such faith,' Piex muttered.

Norius smiled. 'Just as you, youngling, are here for reasons that go far beyond your uncle's cunning plans, too. There is a *reason* these things **had** to happen. Have faith.'

'No,' said Eclipse. 'And if you do not have the sense to free yourself, I will!'

With that, she tore herself into her dragon form. The mother pulled back in surprise, perhaps seeing for the first time that her child truly was half rot dragon. But without pausing Eclipse grasped the chain in both claws. Then she fell back, cut terribly, crying forlorn tears.

'Child, stop,' her mother ordered.

But Eclipse did not stop. Instead, she reached out and grabbed the chain with her teeth. The silver spiked links seemed to twist and writhe, cutting her on the snout. The shining chain clinked with diabolical mockery as the young dragon fell back.

'Enough,' her mother roared in pity and strength.

Eclipse slithered away in defeat and curled her cut snout up under her mother's arms. Then, time seemed to hesitate, and the room filled with hope like the morning breeze at the promise of a good day, and in a moment all of Eclipse's wounds were healed. She looked up at her mother in wonder and surprise.

'I have been saving that prayer for eleven years,' she sighed.

'You mean, you had it all that time, and did not use it on yourself?' Kialessa asked in disbelief.

'Of course not. This chain prevents me from regaining my prayers of power. And there was no point healing myself, it would only wound me in the next moment. I knew–'

Eclipse burst into tears again. 'Mother, no, you must heal yourself. You must remove the chain!'

'I cannot,' Norius said. 'The magic Tobiuus has wrought is too strong. But he cannot keep me here forever.'

'But why does he keep you at all?'

'I honestly think he enjoys my suffering. It gives him a sense of power to have overcome a moon dragon. Tobiuus is evil.'

'But … there is no good or evil,' Eclipse argued forlornly from teachings of the only dragon teacher she'd ever had, her father.

'There are relative good and evils, yes, but also absolute good and evil.'

'Then what does it mean to be evil, mother?' She did not seem to want to hear the answer.

'Evil is simple, child. To do evil is to do what you

know to be wrong.'

'But … what about the trolls? They think anything they do is right.'

'No, they don't. That is a lie. First, even the most barbaric civilisations have many rules about what is right and wrong. Second, even more importantly, every living creature has an internal compass, a conscience, that tells them when they are in the path of evil. They will know, until they oppress their inner conscience, what is right and wrong. And if they do not know, they are not held accountable and it is not an evil act, though it would not be so counted to those who knew better.'

Eclipse was silent, her brow furrowed as she appeared to be fighting an internal battle against years of knowing only lies. Kialessa didn't know what thought helped make up her mind, but she was looking down at the chain in horror and disgust.

'Then there is an absolute evil,' Eclipse pondered. 'I was wrong, Tobiuus *is* evil. He *knows* what he's doing is wrong, but justifies it in his own mind. He must be stopped.'

Eclipse grew angry again. 'If he will not release you, I will pry the key from his dead fingers!'

There was movement outside the dungeon door.

'No daughter,' Norius pled. 'You must not succumb to blind rage. It will lead you to evil.'

'Perhaps, but it *will* bring about change,' Eclipse argued, spreading her wings in resolution.

'Evil cannot change evil, and two wrongs do not make a right. If you battle Tobiuus, you will fall, and I have only just found you. Visit me often, and I will teach you of the ways –'

'Ways which got you into this dungeon in the first place,' Eclipse hissed. 'If you will not fight Tobiuus, then **I will!**'

Eclipse the dragon leapt, crushing the door with a single bounce. Several goblins were in the room and she breathed on them. Not the moon dragon's breath of harmless paralysation, but the rot dragon's breath of decay and despair. Their screams filled the dungeon.

'Stop her,' Norius said, 'or she will die! Tobiuus is too powerful, even if she catches him during rest. Tell her that all trials must be seen through to the goodness they are intended to bring! Tell her that if she allows vengeance to motivate her, then her enemies will control her even after their death.'

An alarm sounded.

'Go,' Norius begged.

Kialessa hastened up the stairs, Piex right behind her. She found herself trembling, and realised she was terrified. Terrified to think of what would become of Eclipse, or of what would become of them once Tobiuus found out. But most of all, she was terrified to think of how she was going to stop an enraged dragon motivated only by revenge.

The archmage and the sagemaster

There are two kinds of trouble in the world, those we can handle, and those we really should keep far away from!
– Humdug – dwarf scholar.

They raced up the tower. Goblins were scurrying to and fro in their panic. Students and servants were everywhere, so nobody questioned Kialessa and Piex as they ran up to Tobiuus's study. But when they got there, there was someone standing in their way.

Dusk.

'Hello,' he said in a crafty voice. 'I've been hoping you'd come. All this chaos, someone could get hurt.'

'Get out of our way,' Piex demanded.

Dusk looked surprised, then laughed. 'Even better!

     By Dr Joseph Ireland "Dr Joe"

You want to challenge me? Ho, ho! What luck! And here I was thinking I needed to make it look like an *accident.'*

'What are you doing here?' Kialessa shouted, hoping to distract them both down before things got magically violent.

Dusk looked at her as if he had just realised she was there, then talked to her just like Tobiuus sometimes did: full of distain. 'The master has had to deal with some kind of intrusion, and asked me to guard this door. No one will get past this door while I guard it.'

'Excellent,' Piex said.

'Piex,' Kialessa begged.

'Stand aside.'

Dusk smiled. 'Just the way I wanted it.'

Piex was the first to cast, his clashing explosion of flickering starlight engulfing Dusk. But the older student dismissed the shimmering with muttered words and laughed.

'You think to best me with that low order spell? Very well, try my wizardry. *Magus sphraerae!'* Three bright green balls of energy streaked from his hand towards Piex's chest.

Kialessa tried to throw herself between the glowing balls and Piex, but they dodged around her and exploded into the dragon boy.

Piex fell against the wall, three deep wounds burnt in his chest. Dusk laughed. 'I'm tired of you standing in the way of my studies.' He begun to advance toward them.

'So I'm now going to make sure you never –'

He didn't finish his sentence because, in spite of the pain, Piex raised a pointed finger and shouted, '*Instanti amico!*'

The older boy stopped in his tracks and blinked as if he'd just been bopped on the nose. When he looked down at them, he looked a little dazed and smiled.

'I really didn't think that would work,' Piex said.

'Oh, hi there Piex, and … what's your name … sorry about that. We must have had a little misunderstanding or something. Here, have this healing potion,' Dusk said in a dreamy voice.

Piex drank quickly.

'You'd better go check on the goblins,' Piex suggested.

'Oh, no. I need to guard this door for Tobiuus.'

'No you don't,' Kialessa said, catching on that Dusk was not quite himself right now. 'I heard he's in the dungeon now and wants to speak to you. To congratulate you on a job well done.'

'Really?' Dusk sounded quite pathetic. 'I do work so very hard. He should be pleased. I'll go see him right now.' And off he went.

The two sighed.

'That's a great spell,' Kialessa said.

'King Dunnkan gave it to me. I finally deciphered it last week. I've been looking for a chance to use it.'

'Let's go save Eclipse.'

Together, they flung the study door open.

***

They were too late. Archmage Tobiuus stood over Eclipse's dragon form as she lay sunk against the far wall.

'I told –' he was saying, but stopped as soon as he saw them.

'What did you do?' Kialessa shouted.

'*Propinquus*,' Tobiuus shouted, and the door flung shut of its own accord. '*Obfirmo*.' A bolt slid across the door. Now they were trapped inside too. 'I admire your ability to rid yourself of my first apprentice, but you've done much to displease me this day, Piex, and punishment is in order. I allowed you to find that dragon in the dungeon weeks ago, to bring a little peace to my prisoner's heart, and this is how you reward me?'

Without waiting Kialessa ran past him to Eclipse.

Tobiuus calmly stood away.

She was still breathing, but only just. Kialessa had no idea what hex or curse Tobiuus had put on her. 'You evil *monster*.'

Tobiuus stood back. He seemed shocked at her outburst. 'She … attacked me, it was self-defence,' he argued, forgetting his own rule not to speak to her again. 'I am not *only* evil.'

'You are *entirely* evil. Why don't you see that the very essence of evil is deception? To take something good and make it seem wrong, then to take something evil and make it seem right! You have become so evil you can't even see it anymore. What have you ever done that is good?'

'I saved the western goblins from starvation. I gave the troll king a weapon to defend himself. I let you visit my prisoners.'

'All things that benefit you,' Eclipse said in a weak voice. 'You call these things goodness? The trolls protect your lands from humans who aren't so happy with your "experiments". And the goblins thank you with free goblin slaves. All your good is for your own personal benefit.'

'No, foolish dragon,' he argued. 'I am filled with both evil **and** good. Do you not see that without death there can be no life. Without darkness there is no light. There **must** be good and evil, and when you harness them both –'

'Opposites are necessary, that is true,' Piex said, his voice unwavering. 'But that doesn't make embracing evil necessary, only real! To say you **must** use evil … it's just another lie.'

'But what is evil then?' Tobiuus mocked.

'You,' Eclipse said, turning her head towards Tobiuus.

'Yes, yes. That's it!' Piex roared in a triumphant voice. 'Evil isn't destruction and disease, though they may be caused by it. Suffering isn't evil, but gaining power or enjoyment though other people's suffering is. Oh, it's so clear to me now. Evil is gaining power or enjoyment from other creatures' suffering!'

'Just like you, Tobiuus,' Kialessa agreed. 'Always gaining power by causing suffering, and then clearing your conscience by doing a few "good" deeds. What do you gain by tormenting Norius? What is it that you gain from teaching Piex to be evil like yourself? What in the world do you want with us!?'

Tobiuus smiled craftily. So there *was* something else he intended to gain by forcing Piex to use evil.

But he did not answer.

'I have solved your riddle, uncle,' Piex said with his newfound forcefulness. 'I know what evil is. Now, **let us go**!'

Tobiuus was calm and composed as he took two steps backwards. 'Oh, I'm afraid you haven't, nephew. You do not know what evil is at all, not at all! But if you choose to fail my teachings, then, I'm afraid, you all know too much. I cannot let you go. Now, unless Piex embraces the true power of evil, I'm afraid –'

Piex stood, and spoke with courage and clarity. 'Evil is wrong, no matter how you look at it. I will **never** turn to evil to gain power!'

Tobiuus stopped smiling altogether. 'I'm sorry you feel that way.' He said, and raised a fist glowing with dark energy. He looked at the three of them, his face a mask of grim determination. 'You might have made a mighty wizard one day, Piex, but just like your father you will not do what must be done to gain true power.'

'I will **never** be like you,' Piex screamed. 'I will **never** embrace hell as my ally. And if I die, I die choosing what is good!'

Tobiuus hesitated. 'So be it,' he muttered, beginning a terrifying spell.

Once again, Kialessa realised there were two kinds of people in the world that you couldn't win an argument against: those who knew too much, and those whose arguments were based entirely on personal belief.

Tobiuus, it appeared, was the second.

But he never completed his incantation, for without warning he was attacked. It was not from a summoned creature, a wounded dragon, or even a magical spell.

It was an imp.

With a screech the imp rushed to save them. Somehow, it must have overcome its selfish, evil nature to find enough goodness to break the chain that held it. Mid-flight, it turned itself into a great red boar, as large as a dog, armed with flaming tusks. It careened into Tobiuus's legs and knocked him clean to the floor, dissipating his spell without hurting anyone.

As quickly as they could they pulled Eclipse behind a cabinet and hid. The imp changed into its natural form and alighted on Kialessa's shoulder. Its leg still had a great gash where it had torn itself free, but it *was* free. Then it turned invisible once more.

Tobiuus stood, dark energy gathering around him.

'You have freed my imp?' He sounded quite surprised. 'I would very much like to know how you achieved that. But no matter, I have no further need of it, or you. Now you all *must* die.'

There was nowhere to run, and nothing to do but pray.

Oh, Eternal! Kialessa thought.

There was a crack, and then a loud *whoosh*. Into the room, imposing himself between the archmage and themselves, was a humble elven wizard dressed in a midnight blue cloak, a glowing purple amethyst on his staff.

'Master!' Piex choked.

'You'd best stand aside, youngling. Your uncle and I have business to discuss,' the sagemaster said casually, as though he hadn't a care in the world.

Tobiuus looked confused for a moment, then laughed again.

'You! You're the boy's castle mage? A lowly castle mage. Do *you* sincerely wish to challenge *me*, an archmage, with your petty skills drawn from the bereft shelf you call a library? Books can only take you so far-'

'Actually, books will take you to the ends of the world and beyond. And I am no lowly castle mage, Tobiuus, I am a sagemaster,' he said, his voice as threatening as it was pleasant. 'And having scryed out your tower for the past three days, I am more than confident I can bring you down, and take you back to the prison you escaped from five years ago.'

Tobiuus's voice was serious. 'We shall see.'

Archmage Tobiuus and sagemaster De'Feur began weaving their first incantations; the shorter-lived protections for battle.

Suddenly Kialessa felt a hand clamp on her shoulder. Behind them a glorious humanoid form stepped from a hidden realm, a giant golden scythe strapped to her back, two huge wings stretching out to protect them.

The angel had returned.

'No,' Piex said, before it could teleport them away to safety.

The angel looked confused.

'I need to see this,' Piex begged.

She pondered for a moment, then nodded in understanding.

Kialessa didn't understand. They were all in incredible danger. What was Piex thinking? The mighty angel helped move them further behind the shelves, placing herself between them and the wizards about to do battle, a pale circle of golden light surrounding them.

'Hold on to me fast, young ones. If their battle turns our way I may be forced to move you to safety without warning.'

'Works for me,' Kialessa said, clutching onto the angel's huge muscular arms. She was glad the angel was on their side.

The wizards fell silent, and at the same moment, made the same gesture.

'What is this?' Eclipse whispered.

'This is good,' Piex sighed. 'Tobiuus has agreed to a wizardry battle. They link minds, and the strongest mind will prevail.'

'This is good?' Kialessa said. 'How is this good?'

'Historically, it means the battle will be civil. They're not out to destroy each other as quickly as possible. This means they may fight to the death, but it will be with honour. At least … I hope.'

The wizards were struggling, beads of sweat glistened on their foreheads, and the room was filled with an eerie silence.

'C'mon sagemaster,' Kialessa whispered.

'How did you find us?' Piex said quietly to the angel in the odd silence.

'Your tae'anaryn friend told me,' she smiled at Kialessa. 'You know, there are many Great Kingdoms within Creation, but only one Piex and only one Tobiuus. I had to travel to the Seeathen oracle, and her price was that I defeat her enemies, but she led me to you.'

'I hope you weren't hurt,' Kialessa said.

'I was, greatly, and I lost two companions.'

'No.' Kialessa's heart ached with sympathy.

'It's all right; they are angels too. Their sanctified bodies have already reformed on the ambrosial realms in the arms of Serros. We are happy to die a thousand deaths liberating those who are wrongly imprisoned, and we have watched you fight for a long time. You are good, young ones, and your deeds make us proud.'

Piex lifted his head with a small smile. 'I was afraid I was becoming evil.'

'We left that choice up to you, and you have chosen well young wizard.' The angel smiled so sincerely it was clear that she was genuinely impressed. 'You have borne temptation well, and it has taught you who you are, and won you the great prize of self-knowledge and understanding. I would not have been eager to stand in your place, young one, and face these tests myself.'

Piex smiled the first genuine smile in weeks.

'How long have you known we were here?' Kialessa whispered.

'Three days, but we've had to wait until the time was right. I was not permitted to intervene until this time and now it is clear to me why.'

'Why?' Kialessa asked.

'So you could complete your testing; you, this dragon, and this imp. And you have all borne your testing with remarkable courage and integrity. I am pleased. Your tribulations have made you great.'

'I don't feel like I've done anything great,' Piex said.

'Resisted the will of an archmage?' the angel said, then peered carefully out from the shelves. 'Though my heart tells me the test isn't fully over yet.'

Tobiuus stumbled backwards, but did not fall. De'Feur laughed, but clutched his staff so tightly his fingers turned white. The sagemaster had won.

Then another battle began.

        By Dr Joseph Ireland "Dr Joe"

Tobiuus stood back and began summoning in his circle, interposed between himself and the sagemaster. De'Feur obliged him by summoning a creature of his own, glistening sigils of protection and power glimmering into reality around him in an instant. A moment later rifts appeared in the air as great beasts were summoned. De'Feur brought in a glowing celestial posk, a lesser angel of the higher realms, flowing with golden light. Yet if the sagemaster had hoped to face a demon, he was going to be disappointed; flames burst into the air within Tobiuus's circle. A being appeared; made only of flames with two clawed arms of fire. An elemental; Kialessa had seen one before, but not quite so large. This one was taller than Tobiuus.

'A summoning battle,' Piex said. 'The creatures will fight, and the loser must face off against his opponent's creature. That the wizards simply stand and watch is the mark of true wizards' duel. Were it on the field of battle, they would not stop casting to await the outcome. They are gentles, both.'

It was a close contest, but in the end the swiftness of the fire elemental won out, and as it fell, the posk disappeared back to its realm.

'It will be all right,' Piex explained. 'Summoned creatures usually only take a portion of a true creature's soul, which makes your appearance here more amazing, good angel. But it means summoned creatures cannot be truly killed outside their home realm.'

Even so, it has been brutally hurt, thought Kialessa. 'But will the sagemaster be all right?'

As if on cue, the fire elemental rushed at the sagemaster. He pulled out a wand and blasted it with a cyclone of ice shards, but it did not fall. It reached him and tried to wrap its fiery arms about him. But somehow, the lithe wizard slipped from its reach and held out an orb. He immediately began a rapid incantation of striking syllables, tendrils of red light reaching out to enwrap the summoned being. The creature of fire roared, raging against its rapidly thickening bands. It took a good few moment, and Tobiuus watched with wonder and respect as the being was inexorably sucked inside the now glowing red orb, soft grey ash falling to the floor around them.

Then Tobiuus laughed. 'So it is down to you and me, sagemaster.'

'That it would seem,' De'Feur replied.

The battle intensified. Tobiuus enspelled an entire cabinet and threw it, books and all, at the sagemaster. He dodged it with the help of advanced *mage's momentum dampening body armour*, and tried to enwrap the archmage with crackling purple lightening. Tobiuus resisted it, then conjured a thundering nimbus of brilliant white energy, but the experienced sagemaster channelled it into the ground harmlessly with glowing motes of dark light. Spell after spell burnt through the air as they tried to best each other. The sagemaster was repeatedly scorched by powerful magic, and the archmage wearied by spell after spell.

But the mages were tiring, their protections weakening.

For a moment the room fell silent as they stood there, grim determination written on their faces. Then, with failing strength, Tobiuus activated a keyword and dozens of tiny pages tore themselves from his books and fashioned themselves into dangerous, sharp beaked paper birds. The sagemaster removed the red orb from his robe and used it to wreath himself in ribbons of fire, scorching any origami adversaries that came too close. But Tobiuus was using the momentary distraction to summon dark energy into one hand, silver energy into the other. The castle began to tremble with the enormous powers he was attempting to forge. An instant later, several other symbols that were lying around the tower leapt from their places. Combined with the clashing lights in the archmage's hand, they had the sagemaster encased in instants, surrounded within an impenetrable sphere of silver and black.

Tobiuus breathed heavily, but grinned in victory. 'Now, let us see you escape from *that* before the end of eternity! Back to business of dealing with the childr-'

There was a loud crack and the sphere began to shimmer and waver. Then the entire image split, and the silver light coalesced around the sagemaster's glowing form. Within an instant the silver light wrapped around the dark light, and dragged it upwards and through the ceiling.

'You …' Tobiuus said.

The sagemaster smiled, a clear orb in one hand, leaning heavily on his staff. 'No, thank *you* for providing the means of my escape. Seriously, how foolish are you in combining two primal forces into a single entity like that? At any rate, this has been a most engaging diversion, but I think we might like to wrap it up now.'

Tobiuus shouted in rage and cast magical bolts of energy at him, but with a swift flick of his wrist and mumbled words, De'Feur appeared to neutralise the spell.

Tobiuus scoffed and cast another spell which the sagemaster cancelled.

'Is that all you can do now, *sagemaster*?' Tobiuus roared angrily. 'Neutralise my spells?'

'It's all I need to do now.'

Tobiuus's magic was almost thwarted as the sagemaster attempted to neutralise another spell, but still somehow managed to fling a portion of blue arcane fire at De'Feur. Whatever protections the sagemaster had against fire at the beginning of the battle must have worn off. He padded the fire that burnt on his robes as Tobiuus smirked.

'And after you, I will find the children. There is no place they can hide, and you cannot keep this up forever, sagemaster. For all your many options I have far more *power* at my command.'

'Well, as I said, I don't need to keep it up any longer at all.'

'What?' Tobiuus said.

The angel turned and smiled at Kialessa.

Then they all heard it. The shouts from below had changed. Now there were clashes of steel and arcane fire, though the noise was muted by the thick stone of Tobiuus's study.

His tower was under attack.

The angel walked out, revealing their hiding place.

'You,' Tobiuus hissed, recognising her in an instant.

She drew her scythe and pointed it at the archmage. When the angel spoke, it was as the voice of judgement, like thunder. 'One hundred of King Dunnkan's soldiers began storming this tower just after your wizards' duel began, archmage. Your students are scattered, your experiments will be used as evidence against you. *Criminal* Tobiuus, you have escaped the lawful prison of your people and defied justice for the last time. Your freedom is forfeit. Surrender now and we will show lenience at your trial.'

Tobiuus was livid. 'Never!' he roared, flying up on his great dragon wings. He began drawing in magic for another spell.

'He's getting away,' Piex squealed.

But De'Feur was prepared. He neutralised Tobiuus's spell with little effort before he could fly away.

Even so, Tobiuus did not need magic to fly, only to fly well, and was already beginning to make his way towards the windows. The angel threw her scythe to the ground where it embedded itself up to the hilt, then ran with great strides towards Tobiuus. With a mighty jump she leapt up high into the air. At the last moment, she pinned him in a mighty wrestler's grip.

Their struggle was brief; a thin and studious half dragon archmage against a trained and brawny angel. Within a heartbeat, the archmage was brought low to the ground. He tried to cast, but the angel held him tight and clamped his jaws shut.

'And just in case,' De'Feur said, before touching his enemy on the brow, removing the delicate wizard's band from Tobiuus's forehead at the same moment that he delivered a spell the break his foe's wisdom.

'Nooo,' Tobiuus wailed, as the light of cunning intellect left his eyes. 'Me, Tobiuus, not wanna be prison. No, nooo!'

The angel, laughing, bound him.

'Now *that's* how a sagemaster casts *Dwenenithak's mental discombobulation*! Very useful, I must say.' De'Feur breathed deeply, smiling in spite his exhaustion. In his hand he now gripped a healing stone the high priestess might have given him. 'I have not had such a thrilling battle in over a dozen years!'

The door to the study burst open, and in rushed four of King Dunnkan's guard. After them came Kialessa's friend Noe-esk, the guard with whom she'd first ridden when they'd taken her to the college. They helped the angel apprehend Tobiuus and secure the area. In the next moment, Darrix, armed and ready, a small cut over his brow, burst in with Allastassia, arcane fire still burning from the two wands in her hands.

'We could not leave them at home if we'd tried,' Noe-esk laughed.

Kialessa ran to embrace them all.

'You would not believe the adventure we've all had trying to find you!' Darrix said.

'All scrying had failed, 'Allastassia explained, while pocketing her wands. 'Then the other day this angel appears in the king's palace announcing that she's looking for people to help release you. They had the whole army mobilised in less than an hour!'

'It was incredible,' Darrix said. 'Did you see the battle with the rot dragons in the swamp? Or were you too caught up here? We had an entire legion of the high king's elite cavalry–'

'Wait a moment, where's Posk?' Kialessa interrupted.

As if in answer they heard, from far down the hallway, the rhythmic thudding of a pair of steel gauntlets against another of Tobiuus's many doors.

'Oh, he's fine.' Allastassia smiled.

'Better go haul him off,' Darrix said. 'Don't want the king's property being damaged any further.'

'High king?' Kialessa asked, not understanding.

'Yes,' Allastassia explained. 'This whole area and its tower have been seized by the king Dunnkan in retribution for Tobiuus's crimes. It is to be turned into a watch tower to help guard the western frontier, once the trolls are thrown out.'

And that was when Posk ran in and wrapped his arms so tightly around Kialessa it made every bone in her back crack. He burst into babble and tears, trying to say something she couldn't understand. So she just patted him on the head, hugged him back, and said, 'Good Posk, good Posk.'

'But what about the swamp? What about the rot dragon, Txlax?' Piex said with great concern.

'We bested it early in the conflict,' Noe-esk declared, chin held high with pride. 'It has fled.'

'Then it can return,' Piex muttered in a sad voice, casting a terrible gloom over what had otherwise been a tremendous victory.

Norius, the moon dragon

I think the greatest good I've ever done was not slaying a dragon or speaking with a god. It was just doing what I knew I should, each and every single day, whether anyone noticed or not.

– Darrix the Devout, from 'Advice to Warriors'.

In the next moment there was a stirring from behind the shelves, and out limped a pale girl with perfectly straight black hair. She was leaning on the arm of the angel.

'Who's that?' Allastassia asked.

'This?' Kialessa said, not to sure what to say, 'is my … friend, Eclipse.'

'Good evening,' Allastassia said.

'Pleasure,' Eclipse replied in a voice as cold as winter.

'Now, if you please, can we return to the issue of finding my mother's key?'

'Oh,' Kialessa said, suddenly remembering. 'Noe-esk, please, we need to find a key to free a prisoner in the dungeon.'

'Wizard's dungeons are no place for children to be.'

'If you don't mind,' Eclipse said like she was an empress, 'But I'd really like to get this dealt with, *without delay*.'

'Hmm,' Noe-esk said, his brow furrowed. 'Well, help yourself, the archmage is secured now.'

Eclipse went up to search Tobiuus's robes. She found several pouches the guards hadn't found, and a ring of keys. But none seemed to her liking. She glared up at the fallen archmage. 'Tobiuus, I know you have my mother in the dungeon. Where is the key?'

He looked puzzled for a moment, but then a cruel smile crossed his lips. 'Key gone, bye, bye. Only with evil heart be freed. Want her wicked, I did.' He gave an insane laugh.

'So you've kept a moon dragon chained up for over eleven years because she wouldn't turn evil? You wicked, evil –' and Eclipse went to slap him, but suddenly the angel shouted.

'Eleven years, you say? It could not be! I have heard of others searching for a Norius, could this be she?'

'It is,' Kialessa said, smiling with rising hope.

'Praise to the higher lights!' The angel shouted in

exultation. 'How many prisoners will be freed today!'

But Eclipse turned to her, her eyes seething with anger. 'There'll be no freeing my mother without that *key*! He tried to make her evil but she'd rather die, and she will die if we don't get that chain off her. It cuts and twists every time you touch it!'

The angel looked serious. 'That is the heart band. That is powerful wizardry. It would not free her if we severed her limb.'

Eclipse gasped.

The angel continued. 'I sensed it when I was first summoned here. I did not think it was in the dungeon.'

'It wasn'ts!' a voice said.

From thin air, a little bird appeared on Kialessa shoulder. They all jumped in surprise.

It was the imp, in disguise.

'A heart band, yes, old magics. T'was the chain that helds me too!'

'That's right,' Kialessa said. 'You were wearing a heart band too, it must have been what the angel sensed. I told you that if you became good, you too would be free, and you did!'

'Most of me, for a moments,' the bird-imp said. Kialessa could still see the cut on its leg.

It was free now, but it did not fly away.

'I know you,' the angel said, looking over the imp, toying with each word like it required great consideration.

The imp looked ashamed.

The angel continued. 'I recognise you. From the time before time. We were once friends.'

'I dids not think you'ds know me,' the imp said. 'Not since we becomes enemies.'

'Look! Look how you've changed,' the angel said in a voice that inspired courage. 'You have touched the light again! You must come with me.'

'No,' the imp insisted. 'Heaven does not want me. I have done great evil, great evil! More than the human minds be imagining. Oh, the suffering. Heaven would not wants me. It would burn me as soon as it seen me coming.'

'Heaven is not like that. It would not teach forgiveness if it did not offer it. If there is a part of heaven in all of us, then I expect they'd welcome you home, no matter what you've done, if you're willing to turn away from the path of evil. If angels can fall, then certainly demons can rise back up to heaven. It is a place of light and happiness and forgiveness.'

'It nice sounds,' Impy muttered.

The angel held out her hand, and after only a moment hesitation, the imp-bird hopped on.

'It does nots burn,' it muttered to itself.

'This is all very nice,' Eclipse said, 'but my mother is in chains even as we chat. Without a key how do you intend to free her?'

'Wait a moment,' Piex interrupted, leaping in his excitement. 'Oh, I get it now! I get it! The rhyme, the poem from the spirit in the test!'

'What about the poem?' Kialessa asked.

'We don't have time for your silly training,' Eclipse said.

'It's the **key**,' he roared, silencing the room. Perhaps he had learnt something from his uncle after all, Kialessa thought, which concerned her just a touch.

Piex recited the poem, word for word.

'Under the tower, silver and black,
A prisoner waits, her freedoms lack.
A prisoner bold, and kind, and true,
Protect her heart from darkness new.
The other chained, in towers tall,
Bitter, vengeful, darkness fall.
Two prisoners, but one key,
Both are trapped, both to free.
Answers simple; for you see,
The one's chain, the other's key.
When once you know, as so one should,
Knowing evil, yet choosing good'

'You got all that from a single hearing?' Kialessa said.

'I did, and it all makes sense now. Who is the first prisoner, the one we need to protect from "darkness new".'

'My mother, clearly,' Eclipse said in her dry voice.

'Good! But the other prisoner? We thought it was you,

Kialessa, but now I see you are not. You may be bitter, and vengeful –'

She scoffed.

'But you're not chained. Not as literally as her mother is. Who here was just as chained as her?'

'Mes,' the imp said.

'Good, yes.' Piex said. 'And once I figured out the difference between right and wrong, I understood how to free your mother. The one's chain, the others key. It's your chain, imp! Your chain will free Eclipse's mother!'

'Of course,' Eclipse declared. 'The spells will cancel each other out.'

'Neutralise, to be exact,' the sagemaster interjected.

'You mean this key?' The angel said, holding out the imp's chain.

'You mean you knew all along?' Kialessa said in surprise.

'Ever since I first heard that Norius was here, yes. I knew only a chain of evil could hold her, and suspected that Tobiuus had already shown sufficient skill at forging such chains. But I was commanded not to reveal it. It was not time.'

'Oh,' Eclipse said in an angry voice, but swayed from her injuries. Noe-esk approached her with a healing potion. 'I cannot believe you'd waste precious time while my mother bleeds for some stupid, unknown cause –'

'Then let us leave this instant,' the angel said, and held the two girls by the shoulders. 'Kialessa, can you get a clear picture of the dungeon in your mind?'

'Not this again,' Kialessa said. As quickly as he could, Piex grabbed on to join in.

'Wait, I – ' Eclipse began, and swiped the potion from Noe-esk's grasp.

CRACK, *whoosh*! They were back in Norius's dungeon, except it smelt like a fresh night in the forest, the only hours before a historic dawn. A bright yellow light burst into flame around the angel's form, and the moon dragon stretched out.

'Norius,' the angel bowed in deep reverence.

The dragon started to weep for joy. Great sobs of relief came from the depths of her injured soul. 'My deliverance. My deliverance!'

Eclipse was injured, but she took the potion in one hand and the imp's little silver chain in the other. Both chains writhed as though alive as they approach each other, and Norius winced.

Quickly, Eclipse dropped the silver chain, no thicker than a string, onto the mighty steel chain with links as thick as a man's chest. In an instant, it had sliced right through the far larger chain like a rock through water. For a moment there was silence, then all the evil in the room fled quick as thought, and the great chain of darkness turned into dust.

The mother dragon roared, then let out a tear-filled sigh of tremendous relief and flexed her arm. Ignoring her own great wounds, Eclipse poured the healing potion onto her mother's wrist, and before their eyes the swelling decreased and the bleeding stopped.

For a moment they embraced.

Finally, the moon dragon's eyes settled on the other two: The tae'anaryn and the wizard's apprentice. 'You have freed me, and you have freed my child. Thank you, thank you! How will I ever thank you?'

'You don't need to,' Kialessa said, and the angel smiled.

'Then I will repay my debt to you by being free to resist evil in this world!' Gradually, her form began to shift and change, and she turned herself into a human, a motherly human with long silver hair and dark silver-coloured eyes. She held Eclipse for a long time.

'Come child,' she said, smoothing down her daughter's hair. 'Let us taste the air and our freedom together!'

But as they turned to leave, Kialessa noticed something in the dust that was once an evil, soul binding chain. Three links, three tiny links of the good chain that had held the imp had survived. Knowing they would be useful one day, she carefully pocketed them while the others left.

No one impeded them as they walked calmly out the tower. The goblins were all slain or driven off, and the other apprentices all captured. Even Dusk, who was causing terrible trouble till Piex showed up. He suggested that what Dusk needed to be doing was showing the other apprentices how to behave by setting an example of how to be a good prisoner. Still under enchantment he was only too happy to comply, and bid them all a happy farewell while shouting out the locations of every secret door and cupboard that he knew existed in Tobiuus's tower.

The solid ground outside the tower was covered with dozens of armed and ready guards, and many of the king's honour guard. They saluted the angel, but did not acknowledge the two women who walked beside her.

'Lumos, my friend,' Norius said, looking up at the dimly lit moon though the clouds. 'How I would love to touch your face once more.'

'Are you well enough to fly, mother?' Eclipse asked in a kind and tender voice.

'Well and beyond, and I will be back to my full strength in a short time. There are many friends I have missed while I've been prisoner, and I long to see them. Including one I hope you may come to know as father.'

'Father?' Kialessa gasped.

'Yes, I have a husband. He has been searching for me, and I want to see him again. Our union has been sorely missed.'

'I must go also,' the angel said. 'I must return to the Sun to report the events of this momentous day to my superiors. I will first see that my services are no longer required by the sagemaster, who was in charge of this day, and then return to run the ambrosial fields for a time.

Your deeds are legendary here, all of you. I will see they are spoken of in the name of goodness for a *very* long time.'

Kialessa laughed. 'We were just doing our thing. You know, trying to make the most of our opportunities.'

'Legendary,' the angel said with joy. 'Come Impy, let us leave.'

Impy hopped onto the angel's arm. 'Warm place for me, no fires!'

'And you have much to re-learn,' the angel laughed, and with a wave, disappeared.

For a moment, Eclipse looked at the sky. 'I too, must leave,' she stated, a touch of sadness in her voice. She turned to Kialessa and Piex. 'I must learn all I can from my mother, and come to know her. You understand don't you? I must leave now?'

'Of course, what are you waiting for?' Kialessa said.

But Eclipse was sad about something. 'You are my first friend,' she said, collapsing into Kialessa's arms and tearing up. 'You taught me how to recognise evil. I will never forget that, no matter how long I live, no matter how long till we meet again.'

'Oh, we'll see each other again.'

But Eclipse didn't seem so sure. 'Dragons live a very long time,' she tried to explain. 'When we leave … and sometimes when we sleep.'

'They sleep for decades,' Piex explained.

'Tobiuus has been accelerating my growth so much I

        By Dr Joseph Ireland "Dr Joe"

don't know what will happen. I feel the time is coming upon me. I must sleep and grow some more. I do not think we will meet again until you are very old, Kialessa.'

Now she understood.

She hugged the girl dragon with all her might, pushing back her own tears. 'Don't worry Eclipse. You have your mother now, and she is good. She will take care of you.'

They hugged again.

'Let us go,' the moon dragon said.

'I will see you again,' Eclipse promised.

'I know it,' Kialessa assured her.

Then Norius whispered a secret prayer of power and a thick fog lifted up from the ground around them, covering all the soldiers there. Only Piex and Kialessa could see the two females shift and unfold their dragon wings, claws and scales. In a moment, the two dragons sprang up from the ground and floated high into the air, the mighty bellowing of the liberated moon dragon echoed by the shill, victorious cry of her half rot dragon daughter.

Kialessa smiled. Great things had been done. There would be such a feast when they returned, and amazing stories to tell about the tower! King Dunnkan had no doubt lost his sleep in worry, and it would be good to hold his hand and walk through his garden in the cool evenings once more. She even realised how much she'd enjoy sitting down at the college and learning all day again.

Kialessa couldn't *wait* to get home!

 By Dr Joseph Ireland "Dr Joe"

Appendix

Piex's study of modern magics

Based on Academiclees' *Great Treatise on the Nature of Nature*, -4 OT.

Two major divisions:

Flow (not opposites, but complementary parts)

Gather – light energy: shine, sound, begin (masculine)

Disperse– dark energy: dark, silence, end (feminine)

Four minor divisions:

Life – health, body, form.

Spirit – time, space, field.

Mind – thought, illusion, enchantment.

Matter – stone (including earth and metals), water (including acid), air (including fire), lightning.

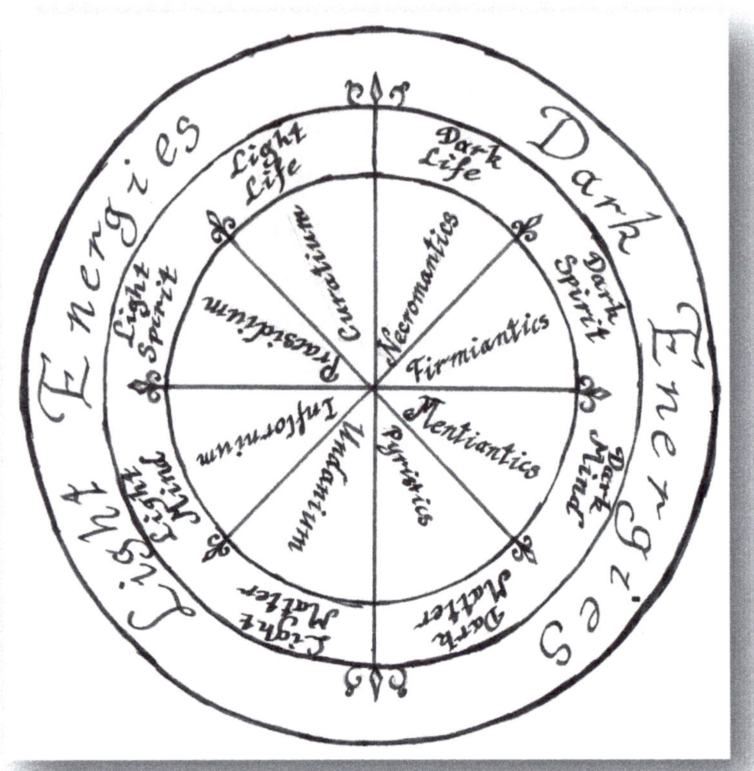

9 The eight halls of magic - by Piex

Curatium –	gathering life – healing, summoning.
Praesidium –	gathering spirit – travel, protection.
Inflornium –	gathering mind – clarity, inspiration, scrying.
Undanium –	gathering matter – construction, healing, illusions.
Necromantics –	dispersing life – studies of death, illness, suffering.
Firmiantics –	dispersing spirit – form and transmutation.
Mentiantics –	dispersing mind – mental control, enchantment.
Pyristics –	dispersing matter – destruction, chaos.

The halls of magic are formed by the combination of the major and minor divisions. To gain true mastery a wizard must specialise in one hall only, and the opposing hall may prove especially difficult to work with. Others pursue different ambitions. For example, an archmage seeks to dominate and command magic as a servant and tool. Others, such as the sagemaster, seek deeper wisdom by studying all knowledge including magic. Note the motif above divides the halls into "light" and "dark", a division many see as artificial. The southern elves, for example, call them the "gathering" and "dispersing" halls, an interpretation Academiclees (2) labelled "glib at best".

Note 1: To say the knowledge presented here is incomplete would be an understatement. In truth, wizardry often suffers from a lack of understanding tantamount to complete ignorance. We are as fools with fire, as they say. Yet wizards are greatly valued in our culture, rightly so, for our deeds are legendary, and necessary to the modern kingdom. But in truth, we yet have much to learn.

Note 2: Wizards debate greatly the necessity of seeing all that is dark as necessarily evil. From my experience the task of good and evil goes beyond what magic can offer, being in the cause the wizard espouses. Thus, evil energy (manifested wickedness) cannot be confused with dark energy (dispersing halls of magic). Even Inflornium can be used to great evil, as it was in the case of the abduction of the tae'anaryn and I in the spring of 313 CY.

Signed – Piex, *the wizard's apprentice.*

Times

Kialessa, 314cy

Day – The period of time when the sun (Serros) travels through the sky and returns to his starting place. Each day starts at dawn.

Times – Each day is made of 4 'times' being; Midnight, Midday and the young boy twins Twilight and Dawn. Of about 3 hours either side of their namesake (i.e., *dawn is technically from 3am till 9am*)

Hours - Each Time has 6 hours each

Moments (*minutes*) - Each hour has 120 moments

Instants (*seconds*) - Each moment is made up of a 120 'instants', which are like our seconds only noticeably faster. Others also use the term 'tock'.

Distances

By Darrix, the prayerful warrior
(Draft – prepared for the arithmetic's tutor)
Based off the measurements of the average adult human.

Length = about as long as the little finger
Hand = about 3.5 lengths, one stretched out hand
Stride or **reach** = about 3.5 hands
Height or **width** = 3.5 strides, height of a very tall man.
Journey = 1750 strides, about a day's journey.

Smaller sizes than a length are usually referred to by their fraction. That is, halves, quarters, eights, sixteenths and so forth.
Other lengths can also be fractioned, but are usually referred to as references. That is, a half distance or quarter stride.

There's a lot of frustration at times that the sizes are arbitrary, and usually refer to the 'average man'. However, King Emerel standardized the lengths after the blood war 300 years ago, and standard measures are available at great expense at most cities.

     By Dr Joseph Ireland "Dr Joe"

Money

1 clay = not much, perhaps a boiled sweet.

1 steel = 12 clay – a drink.

1 bronze = 12 steel – a good meal.

1 silver = 12 bronze – days wage for a skilled servant.

1 gold = 12 silver – more than a fortnight income.

1 bismuth (rainbow bronze) = 12 gold – average annual income for a professional (1/4 this for a serf or servant).

1 zol (clear like diamond) = 12 bismuth – a home, or set for life.

Coins are produced legally in each of the kingdoms of the high kingdom on a regular basis. Official coins bear the regal monarch of the High Kingdom on one face, and the local monarch or emblem on the other face. Counterfeiting money is dangerous, illegal work. While rare, it does happen.

Coin value is determined by weight. Official minted coins are trusted to be their exact weight and quality, while nuggets and other coins may not be and must be tested at money lenders or silversmiths and the like. It is worth noting that the coins are small, about the size of a thumb tip.

It is generally assumed, for religious reasons, that the various materials are in abundance on our world at a 12 fold increase. However, it is now widely accepted that silver is disproportionately available, so one can potentially get richer on silver than gold. Zol is disproportionately unavailable, and attempts to make it worth 13.9 bismuth but are as yet unsuccessful. Zol is known to not be a metal, but it is malleable, an insulator, and holds enchantments extremely well. Gold is a fairly common metal, and most families have several solid gold items in their possession, most notably wedding rings and sacramental cups. All coins are also officially available in:

- "The Half". A coin split in half, usually ignored or given as payment to hated employees. Most counterfeiting stems from this practice of cutting coins in half inaccurately.
- "Two" A twice sized coin, double the weight. Often used. AKA, the "two steel" for a loaf of fresh bread.
- "Three" A three sized coin, broader and triangular. Rarer.
- "Six" A six sixed coin, doubled circumference, commonly used.
- "Nine" A nine sized coin, with 9 sides. It is heavy, and often unappreciated.

The brief attempts of the dwarven nations to create a "four" were wildly unsuccessful, perhaps because it involves diving by three and folks just aren't used to doing that.

(PS. It is also worth noting that most magical items begin their pricing at around 300 gold coins, which is about the price of a home. Wizards and kings demand quality at all times).

Seasons

By Allastassia, the Enchantress
(Draft - Prepared for the tutor of the Natural Lore class.)

Lenmer'el is beautiful all year round. There are four seasons, and each season has ninety-one days with an extra day added to spring and autumn. Every second year has an extra day of winter, considered bad luck. Each season is marked by its middle (forty-fifth day) falling on the equinox or solstice. (By the way, debate *abounds* if the year is exactly 366 and a half days long, as most assume. Like it matters. If it bothers you go ask a wizard. I just talk to the trees to find out what season it is. They're very honest, you know.)

Spring – time for planting. Days are becoming longer than nights. My hair turns auburn and curly, with occasional manifestations of birdlife. The biggest festival of the year, the spring festival, celebrates the first harvest and measures the expected bounty of the new year. (Kialessa and Piex missed it this year, through no fault of their own!)

Summer – warmest season. Hair can be expected to be long and golden. Days are longer than nights. Longest day marks the summer solstice, when the sun is also at its highest point in the sky for the year. The midsummer party tries to remind people to play as well as work, and jokes are traditionally played on each other around this time.

Autumn – the land prepares to rest for winter, a few plants lose their leaves to become dormant. Hair becomes flaming ginger and completely unmanageable some years. Nights are becoming longer than days. The late autumn celebration marks the end of most harvests and strives to kick off winter on a high note.

Winter – coldest season. My hair turns white and straightens out. As for the rest of you, snow can be expected mid-winter, though not for more northern countries, excepting the nations around Pierlou (because of the dragon). Nights are longer than days. Shortest day marks the winter solstice, sun is also at its lowest point in the sky for the year. The winter eclipse, a strange and unwelcome time for most, occurs around this time. The mid-winter festival shortly thereafter, which usually occurs indoors, involves giving gifts and the historical celebration of generosity in scarcity marks the end of the year.

       By Dr Joseph Ireland "Dr Joe"

Dragons of the world

Compiled by Piex

(Draft - Prepared for the
tutor of the Natural Lore class.)

There are three main classes of dragons known to scholars of the Great Kingdom:

Sky dragons – rumoured to be primal remnants of the creation of the world, sky dragons are long, snake like, with four to six claws, no wings and large horns or antlers. They appear to fly by magic through the air as a snake might glide through water. They are almost all associated with the forces of good; however, some have been known to be quite vengeful, dismissive or avaricious. All sky dragons have a human form.

Nature dragons – created by Animas during the first creation, these have four limbs, large, bat like wings, and modest tails. They live to protect or create specific environments, such as forests or deserts. They all exhibit chameleon-like abilities, especially effective in their native environment, where they can be almost undetectable. They sometimes seem to prefer empathy over verbal forms of communication, and demonstrate little difficulty communicating or summoning beasts native to their environment. Nature dragons generally show as much concern for sentient beings such as humans as they do for all other life, though they can be drawn into a conversation if sufficient respect is shown.

Fell dragons – made of an almost infinite diversity of shapes and sizes, most are wretched, twisted abominations of misshapen and impossible forms. Each possess almost demonic powers of evil; rot, pain and thirst, to name a few. Insatiable murderers, these vile beasts seem to thrive on the suffering of others. Most possess a spirit or ghost form in which they are nigh impossible to attack. While in spirit form they cannot attack others, but they can still influence their environment in evil ways. They are believed to be a result of an evil god's perversion of nature or good dragons.

Dragons consider themselves superior to all other forms of life, and in many ways, they are. To a good dragon, this means caring for the lesser forms of life and helping them progress. To a nature dragon, this means insisting on treating all other life as equal, for example, giving no preferential treatment to humans just because they have long memories and can wield axes. To Fell dragons, it means oppressing all other forms of life into servitude or slaughter.

Dragons take between five and twenty years to grow

to maturity, after hatching from an egg bathed in their element or environment for up to fifty years. A newly hatched dragon is ready for battle within hours, but few are truly threatening to humans until at least a few days old. Dragons live to be about a thousand years old, though some are known to double that if they have a particularly compelling cause to uphold.

Dragons possess a unique organ next to their hearts known as the *elementarum* which allows them to breathe out their elemental powers, such as fire. All dragons are known for their capacity to breed with other creatures, usually resulting in half breeds. The 'pocket' dragon, for instance, is the rumoured offspring of an insect and a forest dragon.

Sky dragons (four known sub-classes)

Sun – possibly only one manifesting as many (may actually be the god Serros). Reported to be iridescent gold in colour, like fire. Extremely strong and powerful, said to have a fiery temper and avid punisher of all that is wrong. They are known to be able to breathe fire, fear, or courage.

Moon – very rare, perhaps only a thousand individuals. Generally silver. Can vary a lot in personality and appearance, from dark as night to almost as bright as day. Generally said to be shy, but dependable of character, known to be supernaturally patient and wise. Often reported to take care or represent a certain virtue in its fullness, such as kindness or forgiveness. They are known to be able to breathe frost, paralysis or calming power.

Star – most common of the sky dragons, diverse in appearance and size. Known colours include blue, white, yellow, orange and red hews (though brown and black have been reportedly noted). Highly knowledgeable and informative, generally take care of an aspect of understanding (water magic, a particular culture's history, examples of courage, etc.) Glass shards, sleep or inspiration breaths have been reported.

Comet – usually similar in appearance to a sun or moon dragon, only smaller. They tend to sociable, impressive dragons that enjoy being the centre of attention. Often seen to represent the need for constant change, they tend not to stay around any place for long. They are known to be able to breathe fire, terror, or healing powers.

Nature dragons (countless forms)

Earth – seemingly made of stone, these behemoths take care of rock and stone. They can move through stone with apparent ease, and know the depths of the world better than most humans know their own hand. Earth dragons demonstrate sonic and earthquake powers.

River – long and sinuous, these dragons rarely make themselves known. They take care of rivers, often passing right through the lands of other dragons, yet seem able to get along with them. The largest rivers in the world can be expected to host at least one ancient and enormous river dragon. They demonstrate water powers and often have a steam breath.

Forest – usually green, and very possessive of their environment, a forest dragon must first be placated before logging can carried out safely in its forest. Forest dragons reflect their protected forest in appearance and personality. They exhibit healing and poison powers.

Wind – the wind dragons are almost all wings, and often take on a cloud-like form in which they are difficult to attack. Wind dragons make sure the air is pure and good for all, and thus are treated well by all other nature dragons. They exhibit whirlwind and electrical powers.

Desert – the bronze-coloured dragons of the sandy deserts enjoy dry air. They exhibit many of the powers of air dragons, but can move through sand like the earth dragons. They are often aloof, preferring riddles or challenges of stamina to conflict, but can battle with the best of them when need be. While their habitat is hot during the day, it is often freezing at night, and desert dragons have breath that reflects this. It can both scorch and freeze at their whim. They have sand and wind powers (favouring desiccation over cloud forms).

Fell dragons

(*ward sign against evil*) For example …

Rot – typically dwelling in a swamp – they have decaying and despair breaths. One such beast, Txlax, was defeated and fled during the battle for the archmage Tobiuus's tower by the king's honour guard of Lenmer'el in 313 CY.

Destruction – typically dwelling in a volcano – they have fire and fear breaths. The dwarf lords of the Iron Tower claim to have slain 'Feuerdrache', a terrifying destruction dragon, early in their nation's history. This resulted in the apparent lessening of the violence of Rotberg, one of the most active volcanoes in their region, and allowed the mining of precious stones to take place far closer to the caladra than was previously possible. Smaller destruction dragons constantly wrestle over the abandoned site now, and it is still quite dangerous.

Despair - typically dwelling in a glacier – they exhibit freezing and hopelessness breaths. The Elves of Pierlou have long struggled against a fierce despair dragon that plagues the mountains to the north of their forest strongholds. During winter they placate the beast with offerings of steel and *poissonvert*, a kind of fish. However, more horrific offerings are required when the beast is in a particularly evil season.

Famine - typically dwelling in a desert – they have famine and illusion breaths. The Blithling nomads of northern Aravah have long struggled to defend their lives and homes from the 'Dybbuk', who is actually a great famine dragon. The past twenty years have been a great time of peace and prosperity for them as Dybbuk slept, but this repose cannot last.

Tyranny – typically dwelling in cities – they have stone shards and cowering fear breaths. Few tyranny dragons exist. Working against all that lives in freedom and peace, they are usually driven off as soon as they are found. Some sources, however, claim they are the most subtle of the fell dragons, and one ancient being dwells right in the heart of Nomer'el, spurring its people to ignorance and wickedness. Few scholars place any stock in such unsubstantiated rumours, however.

The cypher

(Given to myself, Kialessa, by Piex, Spring 313 CY)

Kialessa,

Given that I was three when I first developed this cypher, perhaps you will forgive me its simplicity. For example, a 'no' can be expressed with a simple 99, 2. The point is that the cypher is based off common knowledge to Lenmer'el, and the absolute provinciality of our people adds an extra layer of difficulty to decoding. I usually write it phonetically, so cat would be 'Kat', and mouse, 'Mows'.

It is possible to break this cypher without the key, so the key is never written down. Please destroy this document once it is committed to memory. - Piex.

A – Number of digits on King Dunnkan's right hand.

B – Age at death of King Dunnkan's grandfather – King Wolace.

Ch – Year of the unearthing of the Tournid stone.

D – Age at death of King Dunnkan's father – King Peyter.

E – Plarros, …. Sage of Lumos.

F – Birds in a pie (the children's rhyme).

G – Days in a year divided by six.

H – Number of days per season.

I – Number of people contained in the word 'me'. (What can

I say, I was only three).

J – Number of years the castle of Lenmer'el has stood by the time king Dunnkan came to rule, quartered.

K – Years taken to build the main keep of Lenmer'el.

L – Baker's dozen, doubled.

M – Amount of silver coins in a gold coin.

N – Years of the war between Emerel and Nomer'el.

O – Number of castle walls surrounding the Keep of Lenmer'el.

P – Years of life by which king Dunnkan began to rule.

Q – Two score halved, minus 1.

R – Nemon was the ___ sage of Lumos.

S – 1 doubled four times.

T – 243 divided by three, thrice.

Th – Years of King Duncan's life in 300 CY.

U – Number of stanza's in 'the Tournid prophecy'.

V – Number of priests in the council of Serros at Lenmer'el.

W – Years, in 313, in which Dybbuk has slept.

X – Number of kingdom's that make up the Great Kingdom in 306CY (same as this year, thankfully).

Y – Number of Elder gods in the old pantheon.

Z – Days in summer, minus three, halved.

Special terms.

Yes – W

No – X

? – 18

! – 14

☺ - 11

☹ - 13

> Each number may also represent its actual number, of course. Cardinal co-ordinates are expressed as north = N, etc.

By Dr Joseph Ireland "Dr Joe"

Teacher notes

The Tae'anaryn and the Wizard's Apprentice asks a difficult philosophical question: 'What is evil?' How would you answer this question? Here are some suggestions from characters in the book. Which resonates most with you?

- Tobiuus: good and evil are opposites, (like helping and hindering) both have power, and the truly powerful embrace them both (page 43).

- Kialessa: evil is causing unnecessary suffering (84).

- Txlax: there is no good or evil, only what you prefer (85).

- Chammah: evil is perversion of goodness and truth (136).

- Piex wondered: there is no evil, only chaos and law. (101).

- Piex later on: evil is to gain power or enjoyment from other's suffering (179).

- Norius: to do evil is to do what you know to be wrong (127, 173).

Here are some other thoughts:

- Kialessa and Eclipse: is suffering evil? Should you cause others to suffer so that you can prosper (84)?

- The Angel: evil people, knowingly or not, often call their works good (161).

- Norius: we all bring forth acts of good and evil until

perfected (127).

and

- Broack: only the answer that holds meaning to you will matter (117).
- Kialessa: don't worry if you can't answer right away (76).

And some general questions on the nature of evil:

- Is there a difference between *being* evil and *doing* evil?
- What is the opposite of evil?
- Will evil and good always exist?
- Do you think some people are 'born evil'?
- Can we *accidentally* do an evil thing?
- Can an evil deed be 'washed away', or is it eternal?
- Can an evil person become good? If so, how?

Points to ponder by chapter

The question

In this chapter Piex asks the question: 'what is evil?' What prompts this thought? Do you think it would be wrong to hunt down a creature if it attacked you just so that it could eat?

The day the wizard went away

Piex was very upset when his favourite mentor and teacher had to leave. Do you think his reaction was justified or a bit of an overreaction?

Kialessa told him to make the most of the opportunity. Did he? What do you think he could have done to learn without a teacher around?

Of black and silver

Kialessa and Piex were captured and taken to a tower where Piex's uncle tries to force him to learn how to harness the power of evil. What is Piex's reaction? Does he try to learn how to be evil? Would you?

Tobiuus claims there are opposites in everything. Do you think this is true? And just because evil is the opposite to good, does that mean you need to be evil to have 'balance' in your life?

Wizardry

Kialessa begins to learn a little wizardry in this chapter. Why do you think her attempt goes wrong?

Do you think she should make an oath not to tell

others the words of power? What is the difference between an oath and a promise? Are promises important?

Conspiracy

Kialessa was tired of waiting to be rescued. Do you think trying to escape was a good idea? Was it better for them to just wait?

Tobiuus claims that if good hearted angels 'took over' the world it would be a bad thing. What do you think?

Dragon training

Kialessa meets a new friend in this chapter: Eclipse the dragon. Eclipse is a prisoner too. What plans does Tobiuus have for her?

Eclipse tries to prove Tobiuus is not evil because he has done many good and helpful things. Do good deeds counteract evil deeds in a person's life, or must both be answered for?

The test

Why does Tobiuus put them through illusionary tests? Should he make them as realistic as possible, even if that means illusionary flesh-eating acid and bone breaking spiked clubs?

Kialessa has trouble with the moral implications of opening someone's sarcophagus (coffin). Would you do this in the quest for knowledge? Should archaeologists and others search through tombs and graves for lessons from the past? What do you think they do with what they find and what they learn?

Test continues

The spirit Broack takes them from the tower to another place, teaching them and helping them think about their plight. They ask him about evil and he doesn't really answer them. What answer does Broack give?

What good is the advice 'you need to find the answer that's right for you'? Is there any wisdom in such an answer, as opposed to giving them his personal answer? On the other hand, when is it better to answer a question rather than letting others find their own?

The dungeon and the dragon

Norius teaches them that evil will lead to suffering and regret in the end, and that goodness leads to freedom and growth. What do you think?

Norius claims that evil causes can only be commanded through the acts of evil – lies, threats, manipulation. What do you think?

The imp

Kialessa told the imp that it could be free, but what did it have to do? Do you think that sometimes the only thing holding us back from achieving what we want might be our belief that we can't do it?

The dream

Kiel arrived to comfort Kialessa and Piex, showing them that there were many, many people seeking for their freedom and praying for their safety. Do you think perhaps in your life there might be people, maybe even people you don't yet know, who care about your safety and are working for your freedom?

The angel

The angel claims that many who do evil convince themselves that they are actually doing good in order to keep doing it. What do you think? Do you think others have 'given up' on themselves, and don't care anymore if they act evil or not?

The dragons

What does it take to convince Eclipse that Tobiuus is

evil?

What does she do about this? Do you think it was a good decision?

The archmage and the sagemaster

Here Kialessa realises that it is the very nature of evil to take something good and make it seem bad, then to take evil things and make them seem good. How often has this happened in your life? Have you ever mistaken something good for evil, or vice versa? Even knowing the nature of evil how hard can it be sometimes to tell the difference between good and evil?

Norius, the moon dragon

The angel was 'told' not to deliver them till the time was right. Why do you think it might have been important that the angel waited three days to deliver them? What had to happen as part of the 'testing'? What might they have missed out on if they'd been saved three days earlier? Do you think sometimes it's better to wait out a difficult time, rather than never have any pain or suffering at all?

How long might Eclipse sleep for? Do you think Kialessa will see Eclipse again?

 By Dr Joseph Ireland "Dr Joe"

Choice, Set Free

Book 3

Messages have arrived from the High King, while secret whispers speak of impending war. To strengthen the High kingdom, new laws are being enacted on the people that some people might see as 'unjust'...

In every disaster someone suffers, someone prospers, and someone takes a stand. Will Darrix keep his oath to honour the High King? Or will he risk jail, or worse, in rebellion?

How *does* someone take a stand for what they believe in?

Place the date and your personal mark here each time you read this book – libraries included!

Why not share your experiences and thoughts with the fandom! Get a grownup's permission and visit

www.DrJoe.id.au

for fan art, sequels, competitions and more!